TWO WEE DRAMS of love

Kiss and Tell
Dunroamin Holiday

GRACE
BURROWES

Cover Design by Wax Creative, Inc

ISBN: 978-1-941419-24-3

Published by:
Grace Burrowes Publishing
21 Summit Avenue
Hagerstown, MD 21740
Graceburrowes.com

Printed and published in the United States.

Published in the two-novella compilation, Two Wee Drams of Love, by Grace Burrowes Publishing, 21 Summit Avenue, Hagerstown, MD 21740.

Kiss and Tell

GRACE BURROWES

CHAPTER ONE

"Scheduled sex! This divorce is about scheduled sex, Mr. Cromarty. I did not bear that man two children, give up a promising teaching career, and move five hundred miles from my family so I could *subsist* on scheduled sex. Scheduled *missionary* sex."

Scheduled sex sounded lovely to Dunstan Cromarty, attorney-at-law. A bit of anticipation, maybe flirtation over a good meal, some guaranteed peace and quiet, privacy. No bringing a lady home on a rare, lucky evening to find Wallace had just used the litter box and perfumed the entire downstairs.

"I told Calvin I'd put that in the legal complaint," Mrs. Almquist went on. "About the scheduled sex. Twice a week, unless Cal was at some accountant's conference. Then I got a rain check. I told Calvin what he could do with his rain checks."

A moment of sympathy for poor Calvin threatened, though Dunstan allowed none of it to show on his face. Seventeen years of missionary sex might try any lady's patience, after all.

Unless the alternative was no sex at all.

"If we settle your case," Dunstan said, "we won't need to bring up those particulars in the filings, and the great majority of family law cases do settle. How old are the children?"

On his trusty yellow legal pad, sitting at a conference table easily four times his age, Dunstan took down the usual information—family of four, one income, though it was a certified public accountant's executive income, low-interest mortgage, tidy retirement assets incubating in a variety of accounts, and—in these trying times, with the marriage crumbling—the Almquists had *no debt*.

"Do you suspect your husband has any hidden assets, Mrs. Almquist?"

"Call me Dorie. Yes, he has hidden assets. Calvin's sense of humor hasn't been spotted in since the youngest was eight, and I'm pretty sure Cal still has a nice ass."

A low, grinding ache started up at the base of Dunstan's spine, for this was going to be one of *those* divorces. "What about financial assets he's trying to keep from your notice?"

"No. Calvin is literally an Eagle Scout. Cheerful, loyal, thrifty, brave. *Missionary.*"

God help the Eagle Scout when his missus craved a three-doggie night.

"Transparency of finances can make a divorce proceeding much simpler," Dunstan said. "Discovery will proceed more smoothly, and the division of assets won't become a quagmire of motions and hearings."

"What's discovery?"

He explained about the documents that had to be exchanged—financial records, check registers, bank statements, tax filings, anything that might shed light on the couple's financial situation, or their fitness to parent.

With the Almquists, that picture ought to emerge fairly easily.

He was delivering good news, in so far as any aspect of any divorce could be good news, but Mrs. Almquist was swinging her foot like she desperately needed the loo.

She was a ferociously well maintained female—tasteful highlights in honey-blond hair, a toned figure showing to good advantage in a teal and brown pantsuit, and nails lacquered to match her silk shell. Makeup subtly minimized the approach of her thirty-seventh birthday, and her shoes would probably have paid for two new tires on Dunstan's truck.

"Do you date, Mr. Cromarty?"

She was also furious and broken-hearted.

"I'm too busy to date and I never date clients or former clients." Or lawyers, or the good ladies who worked at the courthouse, which left...Wallace and the remote, most Saturday nights.

Sometimes he'd liven things up with poker night at Trent Knightley's, but the camaraderie among the three Knightley brothers had a way of hollowing the bonhomie the gathering was intended to create. For Dunstan had brothers of his own, far, far, away.

"I wasn't hitting on you," *Dorie* said, though her expression suggested she'd consider him for escort service. "You're good-looking, in a tall, dark, handsome, green-eyed way. I was wondering what it's like *out there*, now. I haven't dated anybody but Calvin for the past seventeen years, and things change."

She'd changed, was what she meant, and some of those changes frightened her.

"You're still married," Dunstan said, kindly, because she didn't *feel* married. She likely felt trapped, betrayed, and exhausted. "Unless you want to give Mr. Almquist the fault ground of adultery upon which to proceed, I suggest you let the dating wait."

In Damson Valley, a close-knit rural community within commuting distance of both Washington and Baltimore, dating was best done openly or not at all.

"I will be damned if I'll give that man anything other than what the law says he's entitled to, and not one penny more."

Oh, this case would be great fun. Drug dealers were a pleasure to represent compared to embittered spouses who had the means to torment each other in family court. Criminals understood the rules, paid cash, and referred all three dozen of their closest friends.

Wallace would be ashamed of his owner for such thoughts.

"Have you considered counseling, Mrs. Almquist?"

"Marriage counseling? Like when you have to tell some stranger all the intimate details of your failed relationship? No, thank you. I might hate Calvin, but I wouldn't put him through that. Marriages are private."

Of course, they were. While divorces…

Dunstan turned over a clean sheet on his tablet. "I was thinking more in terms of giving you emotional support to help you sort through your situation. Divorce can be daunting, and some therapists specialize in assisting couples through the divorce itself."

Devastating was the honest term.

Her foot went abruptly still. "I'm not a whiner, Mr. Cromarty. Ask my spin class. Full speed ahead and get the hills behind me, that's me."

"Then my first job will be to contact Calvin's attorney and ask if he or she will accept service of process on your behalf."

The foot started up again. "He's hiring some woman. Women attorneys make less than men, on average, according to Calvin, and he gets off on pinching pennies. I wish just once he'd pinch my behind."

How plaintive she sounded. Heaven defend the good bachelors of Damson Valley when Dorie Almquist's divorce became final. Might be a good time to nip back to Scotland and spend a few weeks fly-fishing, sipping whiskey, and dandling wee baby cousins.

"Do you happen to know the name of your husband's attorney?"

"She had a dull name, like a third grade teacher."

Which narrowed matters down not at all. "Hannah Stark is a new associate with Hartman and Whitney, though I doubt she'd be taking her own cases yet."

"Not Hannah. Judy something, or Jane. Jane—that's it. As in plain Jane."

If the woman made another comment about missionary sex, Dunstan would hand her back her retainer check, though it would pain him to turn away business.

"Jane DeLuca?"

"That's it. Plain Jane DeLuca. I'll bet she wears sensible shoes, with a name like that."

"Ms. DeLuca is a fine attorney, very professional. I'll give her a call this afternoon."

Mrs. Almquist left in a flurry of fruity perfume and indignation, while Dunstan took his notes back to his office and popped a couple of aspirin before his back started howling at him.

He'd never before taken a case against Ms. Jane DeLuca, but by reputation she *was* very professional—for a land-dwelling shark—and even in the courtroom, *especially* in the courtroom, she wore stilettos.

* * *

"What will this divorce cost me?"

The clients always asked, as if the model without the chrome hubcaps might be the better deal.

Jane DeLuca, Es-flipping-squire, always had an answer for them.

"The cost of your divorce depends on four variables, only one of which you control."

Oncologists and attorneys had a lot in common. Both learned to talk about awful truths, right down to the clinical details, without touching on the awful emotions. Too bad nobody ever made that plain to law school applicants until after the loans had come due.

Calvin Almquist adjusted a gold and onyx cuff link that looked like it might commemorate graduation from some Ivy League university.

"Those four variables are?"

Jane launched into the standard spiel, of which Calvin would retain about a third, if he was like most clients enduring the trauma of inchoate divorce.

"So you're saying I can't control the legal complexity of my case, I can't control my spouse, and I can't control whom she chooses to represent her, but I can control my own behavior."

That would be a stretch, given that divorce made brokenhearted, angry fools of most mortals.

"You choose our litigation objective, Mr. Almquist. If you want sole custody, I'll go after that, hammer and tongs. If you want this divorce wrapped up quickly, then you may see your children only every other weekend, but we won't allow the case to get bogged down in litigation. If a cordial relationship with your ex is the highest priority,"—Calvin winced, tellingly—"then this might take forever, and you could still see your kids only every other weekend, but cordial it will be. You choose the objective."

"I want to have enough to live on, but I need to be a father to my children, too."

Which—surely a coincidence!—was exactly what a solid marriage often fostered.

"Both of those goals are sensible and important. You may need to choose between them."

Rather than prattle on about the court calendar, the procedural details—yes, a divorce was a lawsuit—Jane gave Calvin a moment to absorb a bit more of his *new normal.*

Which had to be one of the most hated euphemisms in the language.

Divorce involved choices, usually between two or more bad alternatives. The first choice, however, after the decision to split, was which lawyers had the privilege of presiding over the internment of the marriage.

"So you can't tell me what the divorce will cost?"

It will cost you your marriage, your remaining complement of innocence, and possibly your life savings—but what will that matter when your children are in rehab?

"I can give you estimates." Jane moved away from her desk to touch the soft, prickly moss in her window dish garden. Calvin looked like what he was: a successful accountant—regular features, tidy dark hair, about five-foot-ten with an "I work out Monday, Wednesday and Friday mornings" trimness. He would read accounting magazines on the stationary bike and have no balances on either of his two credit cards.

Jane used a porcelain Eeyore pitcher to water the dish garden, then topped up a bouquet of yellow and pink tulips Louise had sent at the beginning of the week.

"You'll bill me monthly?"

"If you decide to give me your case, and if I decide to take it, I will bill you against a retainer."

When she got around to doing the billing. Louise, the traitor, had always handled that aspect of the business.

Calvin stood, jingling the change in his left pocket. "But you can't tell me what it will cost, how long it will go on, or what the outcome will be. I hate this, and none of it is my fault."

No divorce was ever anybody's fault, not until some time had passed, a good therapist or two had gone to work, and the judgments were all final.

Jane put Eeyore on the credenza, a reminder that he needed a refill.

"Think of this divorce as a disease, Mr. Almquist. You may have done nothing to deserve it, but if you don't take the situation seriously, you will not like the outcome."

Though Jane had never met the couple comprised of a blameless angel married to an irredeemable devil. Still, she sympathized with Calvin, who probably hadn't done anything *on purpose* to sabotage his marriage. He'd be both bewildered and ashamed to find himself in a lawyer's office for anything other than the drafting of a will.

"Is the retainer negotiable?"

Five years ago, Jane would have taken that bait. She would have returned to her desk and asked him how much he could manage, while she drove on bald tires and had no health insurance.

"I'm good at what I do, Mr. Almquist. If I represent you, you will get good value for your coin. Neither one of us wants you wondering if my zeal in the courtroom is affected by the outstanding balance you owe me. The retainer is not negotiable, and may I point out, that retainer would buy you a lot of marriage counseling."

He left off jingling the coins. "Dorie won't go for that. She has her pride, and she's an excellent mother. She and I have managed seventeen mostly good years. We'll manage this too."

"Are you sure this isn't just a rough patch, Mr. Almquist? Seventeen years is a notorious spike in the chart for divorces."

"Dorie is sure. Frequently in error but seldom in doubt, like the British monarchy. I used to love that about her."

Dorie had probably loved that Calvin was on top of every penny, all the time, rather than a lackadaisical spendthrift like, for example, her own father.

Calvin pushed thick glasses up a nose that would have been nice, if he weren't making a not-nice-at-all face.

"Dorie won't like you one bit. She's insecure about her looks and her education, and you're pretty *and* well educated."

He made Jane's red hair and blue eyes—tired blue eyes—sound like a walking affront to the decency police.

"If Mrs. Almquist attempts to antagonize me, that can work to your advantage."

He resumed his seat, laid a steel briefcase across his lap, and snapped the locks. "How much did you say the retainer is?"

He had a checkbook out, a sign not of sound decision-making ability, but rather, of a man who found every moment of the discussion acutely painful, if not infuriating.

"We need to go over the retainer agreement first," Jane said, gently, gently, because this guy had *high maintenance* written all over him, *if* she decided to represent him.

Which she would, because Louise had left the practice, while the rent bill still occupied a place on Jane's payables ledger.

Calvin tolerated the next hour well, despite Jane's misgivings, and thus she did, eventually, agree to represent him. His documents would be organized and timely produced, his check would not bounce, and he'd likely keep his pants on for the duration of the festivities.

A family law attorney learned not to expect much from her clients.

"When will we file?" Calvin asked.

We. Already, Jane had been promoted to *we* status, with Calvin her wingman in the halls of justice, though the last time he'd been to the county courthouse had probably been to buy his marriage license.

"I will meet with you on Friday and have a draft petition ready by Tuesday, though I warn you, couples do reconcile, Mr. Almquist. Seventeen years is a lot to walk away from, especially when you have children to consider. If you do get back together, the unused portion of the retainer will be returned to you."

For an instant, sheer misery shone out of Calvin's brown eyes. He wasn't Jane's type—she didn't have a type—but once, long ago, dear Dorie had thought those eyes attractive. Intelligent, at least, which counted for a lot with some women.

"Until Friday, then." He stuck out a hand, and Jane shook, because business civilities in the midst of domestic tragedy comforted some clients.

"Call me if you have any questions," Jane said, seeing him to the door. They all had questions, and who could blame them?

Speaking of which. "Did you say who Dorie's attorney is, Mr. Almquist?"

Calvin took his raincoat off the coat stand and fit a beret onto his head. "Dorie retained some guy named Dunstan Cromarty. I think he's Scottish."

"Mr. Cromarty is Scottish, also very professional. He'll advocate for Doreen zealously within the bounds of the law."

And from what Jane had heard, Cromarty would be a perfect, if entirely civil, pain in the ass about it, every step of the way.

* * *

One of the law clerks had asked Jane why she preferred to work in the law library when she'd already memorized the entire Family Law Article of the Annotated Code of Maryland.

"Because you never know when you might need to start on Courts and Judicial Proceedings." She'd memorized only certain articles because she referred to them constantly.

The kid had backed away. *Backed* away.

"I was told I'd find you here." Dunstan Cromarty stood before the table Jane had taken over in the Damson County law library, his battered leather case in hand.

"I like books," Jane said. She was prepared to not like Dunstan Cromarty, though he nicely filled out a medium-blue three-piece suit that had to have been hand-tailored. "Stop looming. If you must interrupt me, then take a seat."

He folded long limbs into a sturdy wooden chair that had likely been in the county courthouse when the Confederate Army had marched by on their way to Gettysburg. "Don't suppose you're working on the Almquist divorce complaint." His burr made even his oh-so-casual question sexy.

She could fence with him, but she'd been talking with other attorneys who practiced family law in Damson County. With Dunstan Cromarty, battles should be chosen, not engaged in for the hell of it.

"And *if* I were working on the Almquist filings?"

He slouched back. "The case will not be pleasant."

Beneath the table, Jane fished for her shoes, but one didn't surreptitiously slip into stilettos. "Domestic cases are seldom pleasant."

His aftershave was *pleasant*. Subtle, fresh, spicy. An outdoorsy scent that went with his burr, which—Jane admitted—she *did* like. Rather a lot. Judges and juries were said to like that burr too.

"The Almquist divorce will be a right stinker," Cromarty said. "I'm hoping you'll accept service of process, though I'm perfectly happy to serve dear Calvin at the gym, in his office, or at his Toastmasters gathering."

Any accent originating in the British Isles gave its speaker an advantage in matters of irony—dear Calvin, indeed. Jane put her computer into sleep mode and folded down the screen.

"Why don't I serve dear Doreen at her gym, or her garden club, or in the privacy of her fifty-five-hundred-square-foot marital home?" If Jane had had her shoes on, she would have stood to pose that query.

"Because Dorie—I'm to call her Dorie—would take it out on her lawyer, as would Calvin, should he suffer the humiliation of public service with a divorce complaint."

Cromarty had directed his irony at himself, or possibly the entire legal profession, while Jane's sweet little smart-pad with a mighty battery gave a soft, cyber-sigh.

"Sometimes, I think having the client accept service in person is better," Jane said, when a simple yes or no might have done. "They need to take the litigation seriously, need to know it will wreck their lives."

"Is that a warning, Ms. DeLuca?"

Drat him. A glimmer of collegial commiseration, followed by a sneering jab. Except Cromarty was smiling. One corner of his mouth had tipped up, and green eyes regarded Jane with as much humor as challenge.

Had she ever seen him smile before? "I'll accept process if you will."

"We are agreed, then. Will you be at the bar lunch on Tuesday?"

Good Lord, was it already time for that monthly ordeal?

"I should be there, though rubber chicken on wilted lettuce isn't exactly my speed." Particularly not if Elvin Gregory plunked himself down beside her again and began with one of his infamous "I once had a case…" monologues.

"We can trade complaints then, maybe do a bit of strategizing."

Her right toe snagged a heel strap, and Jane began wiggling her foot into the shoe. "I'm opposing counsel, Cromarty. What will we strategize about?"

"Scheduling, if nothing else. This case will fall across the winter holidays, and I like to go home to Scotland for Hogmanay."

A little bend, a yank with her index finger, and the right shoe was on. Now for the left.

"What's Hog Many?" And where was home, exactly? Scotland, but where in Scotland? Where, for that matter, was her left shoe?

"*Hogmanay*. New Year's. We set great store by new beginnings in Scotland. So many of us have had to make them. Did you just caress my foot with your toes?"

She had. "Of course not. Your foot got in the way while I'm trying to find my shoe."

He reached a long arm under the table and—"Watch it, Cromarty!"—came up with Jane's left shoe in his hand.

"Interesting." He studied the shoe, an elegant aubergine four-incher Jane had bought for a steal at a consignment shop in Rockville. "These cannot be comfortable. One wonders how you march about the courtrooms in them with such apparent ease. Bad for the knees, these things, and they lead to bunions."

The shoes were dead sexy. Not do-me shoes, but I-might-*let*-you-do-me-*if*-you're-really-good shoes. That Dunstan Cromarty was inspecting Jane's shoe at eye level was not comfortable.

Jane used the law library because people frequented the place. People who might pass the time of day with her, or need a hint where the Atlantic Second Reporters were shelved. People who made quiet, comforting people-nearby noises without troubling her. She'd have to find somewhere else to work that didn't leave her open to attacks from Highland shoe pirates.

"Give me my shoe."

He hesitated a single instant before passing over the shoe, the smile becoming a damned dimple in his left cheek. "We aren't truly about to wreck the Almquist's lives, are we, Ms. DeLuca?"

She jerked the shoe on, though the strap was twisted when she straightened. "No, we are not. They've already seen to that themselves. Now, if you'll excuse me, I have a complaint for limited divorce to draft."

He rose, the only guy in the Damson County bar association who carried off a three-piece suit, matching tie tack and French cuffs as if that was simply what one wore.

"I'll be at work on the complementary accusations from Mrs. Almquist and look forward to seeing you Tuesday."

He sauntered off, the view from the back being elegant, strong, and... Elegant and strong were bad enough. Cromarty played fair, but he played to win. Mrs. Almquist had chosen her advocate well.

Mr. Almquist had chosen better, though, because when it came to divorce litigation, Jane wasn't *playing*. She'd make it a point to sit next to Mr. Cromarty at lunch on Tuesday, the better to impress that upon him.

She collected her effects and rose, then nearly fell on her backside when the strap to her left shoe broke.

* * *

Scotland was usually five hours ahead of Maryland, which meant Dunstan often talked to his mother directly after lunch. Mum liked to watch her shows on the telly, and yet, if she didn't periodically get in "a good natter" with her prodigal son, she fretted.

"So mind you don't embroil me in one of your appellate arguments," he told Trenton Knightley, another family law practitioner whom he occasionally opposed. "I've work to do this afternoon, unlike you lot."

Knightley got the door to the Steak and Anvil, where the bar association gathered for its monthly lunches. "Do you think my brothers would allow me to malinger here over expensive beer and tough steak when I could be back at the office, clocking billable hours?"

Rubber chicken and wilted lettuce for some.

"The shoe is likely on the other foot, Knightley. You herd your brothers back to the office, though why we must have a speaker each month is beyond fathoming."

Knightley wiggled dark brows. "We're supposed to finish planning the details of the bar association's Christmas party today too. Have you been a good boy, Cromarty?"

Americans and their endless self-disclosure. "Very good, though it's none of your ruddy business. Shall you do the motion on the Baxter guardianship or shall I?"

The hostess waved to the banquet room, which was about the size of Dunstan's garage.

"You consent to naming the daughter guardian of Baxter's person?"

"I defer to the court. Any one of the children would serve competently. Send me the draft order before you file the motion, though."

"You have issues with trust, Cromarty," Knightley said as they reached the banquet room. "I'll have the order to you by the end of the week."

Every competent attorney had issues with trust, as well as a fine command of language, at least when on the clock. Trent Knightley was a good fellow, and yet, two heads were better than one when it came to drafting court orders.

"Your brothers are waving you over, Knightley." James and MacKenzie Knightley, the corporate and criminal specialists in the Knightley brothers' law firm, were drinking imported beer at the end of the middle table. Both were agreeable men and superbly competent in their fields.

"Sit with us. We'll break into a chorus of *Jingle Bells* when Elvin Gregory starts holding forth on."

They would, too, and probably make it harmonize.

"I'm promised to Ms. DeLuca, though thank you."

"Poker on Saturday," Knightley said, saluting his brothers. "Mac's springing for the pizza, and it's your turn to lose."

Dunstan did not wave to Ms. DeLuca, who'd taken an end seat at the far table. She had her little computer out of its pink case, not a laptop, but one of the smaller varieties made for people with small hands, perfect eyesight and untreated compulsive tendencies.

"Ms. DeLuca, I have it on good authority this gathering will degenerate into a planning session for the annual bar Christmas party, which I will not be attending. Might I convince you to join me in an elopement?"

She slapped her computer closed and jammed it in an oversize shoulder bag, from which a pair of manila legal briefs peeked, one of which was labeled "Almquist, Calvin."

"You didn't mean that the way it sounded," she said, rising. "You can't help that you still don't speak American, but yes, I'll *elope* with you. Just don't tell our clients."

She preceded him through the private dining room, and yes, Dunstan watched the part of her a gentleman shouldn't watch in public. A glance around the room confirmed that the Damson County Bar Association was sadly lacking in gentlemen, and the ladies present were not surprised to find it so.

Both Dunstan's mum and Wallace would have been ashamed of him, but his brothers and cousins would have understood.

He held the door for Ms. DeLuca, a short exercise in confusion on her part and patience on his, and then they were outside on a pleasant autumn day. Yellow leaves scraped along the sidewalk, and sunlight slanted sharply through bare branches overhead.

"Where are we eloping to?" she asked. "I have the Complaint for Limited Divorce, but I'm also hungry."

She wasn't simply American, she was Jane DeLuca: Here's your lawsuit, I'll take fries with that.

"I have Mrs. Almquist's too, though I'm not sure filing this soon is the appropriate approach. Will you share an Eritrean meal with me?"

Because Eritrean fare—a rare treat in rural Maryland—done right was a wonderful break from sandwiches consumed standing up in the kitchen after the cat had been fed. Even Ms. DeLuca's dubious company couldn't douse Dunstan's longing for a culinary change of pace.

"Haven't had Ethiopian since I moved out here from DC," Ms. DeLuca said, marching off across the street. "A good dose of carbs sounds perfect, and why shouldn't we be filing complaints, getting the ball rolling, starting discovery?"

He hauled her back by the strap of her purse as an orange scooter came barreling around the corner, and in her fancy shoes, she teetered for a moment, then righted herself.

"A simple, 'watch your step' would do, Mr. Cromarty."

"I beg your pardon." The dratted woman would injure herself in those ridiculous shoes, and why did she bother with them, when even in her heels, she came only to Dunstan's shoulder?

This time, she looked both ways before proceeding, and let him hold the door for her when they reached the restaurant.

"A table or a booth?" the hostess asked.

"Table," from Ms. DeLuca, of course.

"I'd prefer a booth, for privacy, and in case we have to spread out any paperwork." Also to be contrary, because exploring the other side's weaknesses was good strategy and half the fun of being an attorney.

"A booth will do," Ms. DeLuca said. "Though you'd better not spill anything on my files, Cromarty."

Or she'd what? Hit him with her Lawyer Barbie computer?

"I'll be quite tidy," Dunstan said, because he was always tidy. The other benefit of a booth—or detriment, depending on a fellow's perspective—was that it mooted the whole dilemma of whether to hold the lady's chair.

"Would Madam like silverware?" the waitress inquired, when they'd settled in a corner booth. She had a musical, slightly French accent, four gold hoops in her right ear, and a friendly smile.

Ms. DeLuca slung her shoulder bag off with the same weary competence Uncle Donald hung up his game bag after a morning's shooting. Instead of bloodstains, her gear sported a pattern of carousel horses in brown, turquoise, and rust.

"We'll be fine without silverware," she said. "Just bring plenty of bread and some spare napkins. Lemon with the water would be lovely too. No ice."

Ms. DeLuca had thoughtfully waved off Dunstan's cutlery, but he wasn't about to admit a partiality to knives, forks, and spotless ties before opposing counsel.

"And I'd like to see your liquor menu," he said, before Ms. DeLuca excused the wait staff as well. "If it wouldn't be too much bother."

He made the request because good drink was an indulgence available even in the wilds of Maryland, but the greater pleasure was seeing Ms. DeLuca's surprise.

"You drink alcohol during the workday, Mr. Cromarty?"

"You don't? For most of us in solo practice, the workday encompasses lunch and dinner, if not breakfast. A wee dram helps the time pass agreeably."

In the time it took Dunstan to open the menu, Ms. DeLuca castled her mental chess pieces. She clearly did not imbibe during the workday—alas, the Puritans had arrived to these shores in substantial numbers before the Scots—and yet her response was verbal sleight of hand.

"For me, whether to have a drink depends on the selection," she said. "We're close enough to DC that a good wine list isn't rare, but rural enough that it's not a foregone conclusion, either. Now, what shall we have?"

Dunstan knew what he'd have—*anything* as long as it wasn't ruddy chicken or tuna fish—but as he stared at the menu, no particular dish caught his fancy.

He was too busy wondering if, beneath the table, Ms. DeLuca had already divested herself of her ridiculous shoes.

CHAPTER TWO

The Annotated Code of Maryland contained no requirement that an attorney bear personal animosity toward opposing counsel in a lawsuit—just the opposite, in fact. Attorneys were at all times to show civility to parties, witnesses, court personnel, and each other—probably to cranky Scotsmen, too—and yet, Jane was nonplussed to find herself enjoying Dunstan Cromarty's company.

His charm was subtle and easily overlooked, bless his wee Scottish heart.

When Jane walked with him, he did not tear along at a speed intended to broadcast to the world, "I have places to go, people to see, snappy repartee to be overheard exchanging!" as many attorneys did. He sauntered along, because whatever places he had to be or people he had to see, they'd wait for him to arrive.

He'd sauntered along on the *outside*, closest to the street, where an old-fashioned gentleman knew to position himself when escorting a lady. Jane's grandma had probably found that bit of arcana on the Rosetta Stone.

Jane liked that Dunstan Cromarty troubled over his appearance—that suit was *not* JC Pen-wah—though he carried a battle-scarred leather briefcase that looked as if some uncle or grandparent might have passed it down to him.

"I'll have the yesiga sambusa and tikel gomen," Jane said. "With lots of potatoes, and don't spare the bread."

"You'll not be having a salad?" Mr. Cromarty asked. "And am I to order for you, then?"

And there was more of his subtle charm, in the guarded quality of his questions. He was curious, but unwilling to offend, though his manners were probably everything his mama hoped for.

"If you order, then I can start planning dessert. What are you having to drink?"

"They've Fraoch here, a heather ale brewed in Alloa, right along the Firth in Clackmannanshire. Goes with anything, and you don't come across it every day."

That was dessert. That bouquet of Scottish places and terms, served up on a bed of casually rolled r's, enunciated d's, fading g's, and softened vowels.

"Where?"

"Clackmannanshire, up the River Forth from Edinburgh. Very pretty, like most of Scotland. Would you like to try the heather ale?"

Because the rest of the Damson County bar was off planning a Christmas party, the restaurant remained relatively quiet. The few other patrons wandering in wouldn't notice Jane's professional detachment turning to mush at the hope in Dunstan Cromarty's voice.

The man was beer-proud of his homeland. "Why not? Is that where you're from, that Cluck-whatever place?'

He didn't wince, but neither did he approve of her mangling the home of his favored brew.

"Clackmannanshire? No, though my younger brother worked there for a bit. My parents hail from Perth, though my grandparents are all from the west of Scotland."

He put about three extra vowels and a spare syllable in Perth. Paireth. Any juror with ears would be spellbound by that accent, though they might not understand some of what was said—not that juries understood everything they heard, regardless of counsel's accent.

Conversation stalled as the waitress appeared with their water and the bread basket. The scent of the warm, vinegary injera was a pleasure for the nose every bit as delightful as Cromarty's accent was for the ear.

"I'll take that," Jane said, reaching for the bread basket. "And we're ready to order."

Cromarty recalled her selections—even the extra potatoes—and chose shrimp for himself.

"I would have pegged you for a beef kinda guy," she said, peeling off several inches of injera before offering him the basket. "I love this stuff. Love. It. Remember that if you're ever trying to turn me up sweet and there's no decent chocolate on hand."

He accepted the basket and set it down without partaking. "One would never have guessed."

Rather than return fire, Jane savored a bite of sheer, gustatory satisfaction. "Doesn't even need butter, and they always bring lots of it." She hadn't had any injera since Louise had pulled up stakes to teach at an art school.

A family came in with a baby in one of those baby basket-seats, the handle ergonomically twisted to ensure Junior could be hauled about everywhere without Mom or Dad's arm getting tired. This model looked like it came equipped with airbags and an entertainment station.

"There goes the neighborhood," Jane muttered, stuffing another bite of injera into her mouth.

"You don't care for children?"

"I like children a lot, but the rug rat will start bellowing here directly, as soon as Mom and Dad try to have an adult conversation. They're always teething when they're that small."

The little family trundled by, the baby nothing more than a pink, sleepy face among soft blankets and padding.

"The bairnie's too wee to teethe yet," Cromarty said, his tone wistful. He turned a green-eyed gaze on Jane as she inhaled another bite of injera. "I admit to some puzzlement, Ms. DeLuca. You're having bread with your bread and bread with your extra potatoes, and I heard mention of dessert. Are you the only American female who doesn't fret about her weight?"

He posed this question without so much as a hint of a wandering eye, a skill necessary if one was to cross-examine witnesses effectively.

Or hide genuine curiosity.

"I like food, Mr. Cromarty, and though I'm usually careful about what I eat, sometimes a good dose of carby bliss can make an otherwise unpleasant chore bearable. Like your wee dram."

He comprehended the analogy, but—let the record show—did not concede the point. "Is carby a word, then, Ms. DeLuca?"

The baby-family settled in two tables away, and Junior uttered nary a peep.

"There you go being Scottish again. In American, when the punch line is *bliss*, some leeway is allowed with the modifiers."

"For a Scot, when the punch line is *bliss*, no modifiers are necessary. Have you any reason not to send the Almquists to mediation over the custody issues?"

He took the injera in one hand and tore back a strip with the other, the way he might have torn off a strip of paper to jot down his phone number. The gesture was fastidious and gave Jane an entire second to shift from carby-bliss to unpleasant-chore mode.

"Yes, I have a reason for avoiding custody mediation. My guy doesn't want to waste the money. Why spend four hours in court-ordered mediation if you know ahead of time you won't get anywhere?"

"A psychic client. How I wish I'd been retained by one myself. I don't envy you." He poured his beer into its special beer glass, letting the beer dribble down the side in the exact quantity necessary to form a foamy head without spilling over.

"Not psychic. Broke. Have you talked money with your client?"

"Some. Shall I pour your ale?"

"Please." Because competence in any regard, but especially when it involved a man's hands, was a pleasure. "The Almquists are trying to maintain a decent lifestyle on one income, and mediation could cost them a grand they don't have. Why don't we at least try to come up with a parenting plan for them? They've already parted with the retainers, and they have only the two kids."

He remained silent while he poured Jane's ale, as if putting beer in a glass was his equivalent of savoring carby bliss. When the beer ritual was complete, he passed Jane her drink, then touched his own to it.

"To a quick, equitable, durable settlement."

"Cheers."

She sipped, because that was what the moment called for, and found... designer beer? "This tastes like flowers."

"The heather is infused. The results don't always turn out this well. I'll ask Doreen if she's amenable to a four-way meeting on the subject of parenting and try to come up with some proposals before we meet with you. I take it we're going forward without fault grounds?"

The Toothless Wonder stirred to life. A small fist waved above the batting and blankets, and a thin cry sounded.

"That child wants a beer," Jane said.

"That child wants a cuddle," Cromarty countered, but softly, and as he spoke, the dad extracted the kid from the space shuttle and cradled him against his shoulder. Junior went immediately quiet.

"Do you have children?" Cromarty wore no ring, but—family law, much?—that didn't mean he wasn't a father.

"Cousins, siblings, nieces, nephews." He drew his finger around the rim of his ale glass. "It's in the Almquists' favor that they don't have fault grounds. Their divorce might not be too bad."

Fault grounds, meaning adultery usually. On that cheery thought, the yesiga sambusas were brought to the table. The spicy, meaty scent went surprisingly well with the ale.

"Have one of these," Jane said, holding the plate of sambusas out to him. He was watching the baby, the infant again in charity with the world and grinning over the dad's shoulder. Jane waved the plate a few inches either direction. "Earth to Cromarty, food's here."

That look passed over his features again, a careful non-reaction that pretty much shouted displeasure. In the courtroom, she wouldn't mind putting that look on his face from time to time. Over lunch, however...

"My name is Dunstan, Ms. DeLuca. Dunstan Lachlan Cromarty." He put one of the meat pastries on his plate.

"Is that an invitation to use your first name?" In this enlightened age, Jane did not presume with the guys in any manner she wouldn't want them presuming with her.

And the Laird of Damson County's Family Law Bar probably wouldn't take kindly to presuming from anybody.

Dunstan Lachlan Cromarty unfastened his tie tack—a gold unicorn with a blue gemstone for an eye—and undid a button midway down his shirtfront. Next, he slipped his tie into the gap in his shirt, leaving the button undone,

Continental-style.

He looked up when he'd finished rearranging his attire to protect his tie from flying gravy, and the sternness remained in the cast of his features, while in his eye…

A goddamn twinkle?

"How does one put it in American? Me Dunstan, you Jane?"

He bit off a tidy corner of the sambusa, while Jane tried not to choke on her ale. Mr. Cro—*Dunstan*—would be a terror on cross-examination, well prepared, quick, to the point, merciless, and blessed with excellent timing. Poor old Calvin wouldn't know what hit him—again.

But Dunstan Cromarty would be a magnificent terror.

If they went to trial, Jane would just have to be magnificent-er.

They tossed around various parenting scenarios for the Almquists, speculated about the new hire working for Trenton Knightley, and found that heather ale went equally well with shrimp wat and tikel gomen.

As the finger bowls were brought out, and Jane fished around under the table for her shoes, she tried to put a name to what wasn't sitting well.

"This is yours," Dunstan said, passing her right shoe over to her, then scooting around to reach under the table again. "If you'll give me a moment,"— warm fingers glided over Jane's ankle and shin—"got it."

He passed her the left one.

"My thanks."

While she put her shoes on, he repositioned his tie and tie tack. The moment had an intimate feel, nobody in a hurry, nobody too self-conscious about dealing with wardrobe matters in public, and *that* was also part of what was wrong with the meal.

"I enjoyed this," Jane said as they headed for the register. "Only another lawyer can understand what the practice of law entails, and I like talking shop, and yet, those bar association lunches—"

"We wouldn't be solo practitioners if we craved the constant company of our confreres."

Missing Louise wasn't the same as craving constant company, was it?

Dunstan had his wallet out in a single smooth-guy move. One instant, his hands were empty, the next—bam!—silver plastic was proffered from a worn black billfold.

"We'll split it," Jane said, fishing in her shoulder bag for her wallet. "Or I can get the sambusas because I ordered them."

The lady behind the cash register hesitated before swiping Dunstan's card.

While Jane fumbled around in the depths of a purse-cum-briefcase-cum-gym-bag that Louise had dubbed "The Vast Lonely."

Dunstan leaned closer, close enough that the difference in their sizes became more apparent than usual.

"Jane, cease yer frettin'," he said quietly. "Next time we have a working lunch, you can have the tax deduction."

Jane stopped rummaging in the depths of her shoulder bag, though she did not *cease her frettin'*.

This informal meal between Me Dunstan and You Jane, this experimenting with heather ale and sharing of courthouse gossip, hadn't felt like a working lunch, though some work had been accomplished.

This meal, with Dunstan ordering, Dunstan passing over her shoes, and Dunstan now holding the door for her, had felt like that most rare and precious of all surprises…

An enjoyable date.

* * *

"I tend to favor mediation," Dunstan said. He'd taken a place across the conference table from his client, the better to protect himself from the aggravation of the scent she wore. "You and Mr. Almquist know your children better than the judge does, you know the family situation better than anybody else, and you are the ones who'll have to live with any parenting schedules included in the court order."

Doreen wore a teal silk blouse—and the teal nails—but her pantsuit was russet, putting Dunstan in mind of… he could not recall what, and it didn't matter, because Doreen had once again accessorized her ensemble with indignation and hurt.

And a baby-powder perfume that made his nose twitch.

"You want us to come up with a parenting schedule," she said, drumming those nails on the conference table. "If it's parenting, then it's down to me. My yogilates class is full of women who get every other weekend off from the parenting schlepp, and I'd be happy to have that much time to myself."

"The children are in school, aren't they?"

"Subtle, Dunstan." The drumming increased in tempo. "Yes, they're in school, and that means I have little more than six glorious, fun-filled, action-packed hours of the day to do the housework, the yard work, the grocery shopping, the laundry, fit in my classes, get dinner started if I'm doing anything besides leftovers, and handle whatever else that might come my way—I've told Cal for the past year we need to replace that water heater, and lo and behold, yesterday morning was wasted waiting for the delivery guys. And then I put on my chauffeur hat."

"While Calvin does what?"

He asked because she needed to tell this story to somebody, and no real work could be accomplished until she had.

"Hell if I know. He goes down the road each morning, and comes home when he comes home. Traffic on I-270 is the other woman in our marriage when tax season isn't holding him hostage."

"So your parenting proposal is every other weekend with Dad. What about holidays, school breaks, vacations, that sort of thing?"

this was why Dunstan favored mediation, because prodding tired, heartbroken, scared people to think about their children, about how the divorce would affect those helpless to prevent it, was in itself wearying and heartbreaking.

His lower back agreed, so he got up and adjusted the blinds in his small conference room.

"The boys gave up on Cal years ago," Doreen said. Around the conference room, Dunstan had hung poster-size sticky notes, a twenty-eight-square grid marked out on each one in black. The squares were filled with red M's and green D's, for Mom and Dad. "And I'm not a dad, Dunstan."

The sight of those damned squares never failed to bother Dunstan. "What if you had a different schedule for tax season and the rest of the year? Mightn't Calvin find more time for his children?"

Her nails stopped drumming for the space of three quiet seconds, then resumed. "He's scared of those boys. They're loud, they're messy, they forget to put the seat down, and they're interested in girls."

"They have something in common with their father, then," Dunstan said, resuming his place at the table to copy the schedules on the wall onto his legal pad.

"Gonads? Gorillas have those. I hear more about junk, packages, and—if it weren't for the Dictionary of Urban Slang, I'd hardly know when to scold my own sons."

And yet, she didn't make the effort to talk to her husband, or had given up trying, and refused counseling. Dunstan was reminded of the quote about happy families being all the same, but troubled ones each having their own tale or woe.

Which thought was interrupted by a prodigious sneeze, followed by a terse "bless you" from Doreen.

Dunstan tended to pinch his nose together when he sneezed, which his mother claimed would cause his eyeballs to explode, though it saved him the great honk of an escaped sneeze. He put his handkerchief to use and scooted his chair back.

"Think about parenting options you can offer your husband, Doreen, the more the better. We're brainstorming now, trying to be creative. I've been looking at your budget, and at the statement of assets and liabilities. You should still consider counseling. Single parenting is hard, even harder than the parenting you're doing now."

She rose swiftly. "Counseling costs money when we're broke enough as it is. I'm not good at numbers. That's why I married an accountant."

And if Calvin thought he was valued only for his accounting, how was he to know the missus was longing for a family picnic or wild, monkey, laundry room sex?

"Money is always a delicate topic when a marriage ends. How do you and Calvin manage it?"

While Doreen wandered around the room studying the various schedules as if they were displays in some contemporary art gallery, Dunstan cracked the window and drew from her a picture of family finances as rigid and distant as the parties themselves.

"So you pay all the household bills from the account in your name, while Calvin manages the investments?"

"I don't understand all that SEP, T-whatever stuff, and Cal thrives on it. He puts a chunk of cash in the household account, and I pay the bills. That way, he doesn't bother me about every little carryout order or heating bill. It's one part of our marriage that hasn't caused problems yet."

She was either ashamed, lying, trying not to cry, perhaps all three.

"If you can have only one part of the marriage functioning smoothly, finances are a good one to have. What does Calvin do for spending money?"

Doreen paused before the window, which looked out over a long, narrow backyard, the office being a renovated row house a block away from the courthouse.

"That is a beautiful oak, out behind your office."

The tree was huge, probably centuries old, and at present a luminous yellow in its autumn plumage. The weather was changing, though, the temperature dropping, the wind tearing at the leaves remaining on the branches. Then too, the increasing chill had turned Dunstan's back twinge-y again.

"Aye, it's pretty, but those falling leaves clog every gutter and downspout for half a block. You were telling me about Calvin's spending money." Or she was avoiding talking about it, though she could linger by the window all morning if it would spare Dunstan another sneeze.

"He has his own credit card, probably one of those business cards in some impressive, glossy finish. I don't bother him over it. All he does is buy gas with it unless he's off to some accounting conference."

Uncle Donald claimed that hunting had less to do with good aim and more to do with the ability to sit still and shut up. Game wandered into view sooner or later, if the hunter could be patient.

"We'll need to have a look at *all* the bank statements, Doreen. *Every* bill, *every* credit card statement. Calvin is an accountant, he'll understand why verification is needed for what's on the accounting filed at the courthouse."

She put her hand on the window glass, her teal nails spread against a backdrop of golden oak leaves soon to fall. "He'll fuss. Is that really necessary?"

Dunstan stayed where he was, enduring a pang of sympathy for Doreen Almquist while an eddy of chilly autumn air rescued him from another sneeze.

She was disappointed in Calvin—or disappointed in life and attributing more than a fair share to her husband—but she believed Calvin was a basically decent fellow she was no longer attracted to.

"Calvin is a CPA, Doreen, and he's keeping a separate account you never see, and though most men in his position would expect to handle the household bills, he's turned that over entirely to you, and he never—not at Christmas or birthdays, not for the yard work or the new water heater—double-checks your work or second-guesses your decisions. That makes me nervous."

She pushed away from the window and retrieved a shimmery, silky, taupe overcoat from the coat rack in the corner. That coat was pretty and likely felt lovely on, but it wouldn't keep her warm when the weather changed, which this time of year was inevitable.

"Good," she said. "I'm paying you to know when to be nervous. I'll meet you here at nine thirty Tuesday morning and go over my parenting proposals with you before Calvin and his lawyer arrive."

"Until Tuesday," he said, getting to his feet. "And please compile copies of the household bills and bank statements, Doreen. The parenting schedule might be easy, but the money could get interesting."

She paused, a taupe silk scarf hanging around her neck, her coat gaping open.

"It's called rehabilitative alimony, right? So I can get back to work, complete a master's degree, maybe get a PhD. A fine idea, but who's going to finish raising our children while I'm recovering from fourteen years of stay-home parenting and Calvin's sitting in traffic?"

She whipped the scarf over her shoulder and swept out, a woman entitled to her petty dramas and parting shots.

But Dunstan prayed to God he'd sniffed the last of whatever fragrance she'd worn today. Most perfumes didn't bother him—and some, say, that favored by Jane DeLuca—he liked—but if Doreen wore the baby powder scent again, he'd have to say something.

And the tickle in his nose was accompanied by a tickle in his memory. Teal was close to turquoise, and Dunstan's mind clicked into recognition: Doreen's wardrobe favored the same colors as Jane DeLuca's carpetbag, though carousel horses and angry housewives were very different uses of the same hues.

He pushed aside his recollection of Jane rummaging in her bag as she tried desperately to prevent him from paying for her meal. Tried and failed.

No more cozy lunches with opposing counsel for him, not when the Almquist case was developing a faint odor of complication and bad behavior.

Doreen maintained her designer wardrobe, designer nails, designer hair, and designer body out of the household account, while also driving an SUV that likely averaged twelve miles to the gallon and four entertainment stations per child.

Spin classes, yoga classes, lunch with the ladies, membership at the bath and tennis club if not the country club… All of that cost money, and Calvin managed to provide for it on an accountant's salary, while also contributing to investment and retirement assets.

Dunstan left the sticky posters where they were, for by this time Tuesday, those draft schedules would sport every color of the rainbow. Despite all the discussion and worry that went into the final product, Calvin would likely end up with every other weekend, alternating holidays, and two non-consecutive weeks in the summer.

Unless he was serving time in a federal prison for embezzlement or fraud.

* * *

Dunstan Cromarty's office was almost what Jane had expected: a *historical* row house, renovated in the nick of time for office use, complete with narrow stairs, creaking floors, and chair rails bearing at least a century's worth of nicks and dents.

The octagonal conference table, however, was magnificent.

"I wonder how many hours Cromarty billed to be able to afford this table," Calvin said, taking a seat. "Maybe I should carve my initials into it for my contribution."

"Don't be sacrilegious," Jane retorted, stroking the rich, red-blond surface of the table. "Chestnut trees in Maryland all but died out when the chestnut blight came through a century ago. My grandpapa said antiques like this are all that remain of a gorgeous and once-thriving native tree."

"That's not exactly true."

Dunstan Cromarty stood in the doorway to the conference room, his suit today a dark, forest-at-sunset green, his tie a paisley in shades much like the polished wood of the table. Tie tack and cuff links matched again, gold with inset amber—a lion this time, not a fanciful unicorn.

He wore wire-rimmed glasses halfway down his nose that, for reasons Jane would examine in solitude, made her wonder what he'd look like wearing *only* those glasses.

"Mr. Cromarty." She rose and extended a hand, because demonstrating to the clients that matters would proceed civilly—*not* speculating about opposing counsel's physique—was the first order of business. "I'd like to introduce Mr. Calvin Almquist. Calvin, Dunstan Cromarty."

They shook, Calvin eyeing Dunstan like a frat boy pledging a rival house.

"Mrs. Almquist and I will join you shortly," Dunstan said. "Can I get anybody a cup of coffee?"

More civilities, of course, though it would be law office coffee, which only night-shift cops or nurses would regard as drinkable. Jane demurred and resumed her seat when Dunstan had withdrawn to whatever neutral corner his client lurked in.

"Is making us wait in here supposed to be a tactic?" Calvin asked, thumping his metal briefcase onto the conference table with about as much regard for the finish as a dog had for the sofa's upholstery.

"We were a little early, Cal. That wasn't a tactic on our part, so no, I won't start accusing anybody of tactics yet." Nor would she speculate any further on whether—twice—Dunstan had touched her foot by accident or by design.

And if by design, had he been trying to distract her from the case?

Mrs. Almquist was like Dunstan's office. In general, she was pretty much as expected: mid-to-late thirties, chilly, wary, tired, and dreading what lay between her and her freedom. She was a bit unexpected too, though, in that she was well put together, right down to lacquered bronze nails, honey-blond highlights, sculpted brows, expert makeup, and a blue silk suit that tactfully whispered outstanding good taste.

She hadn't let herself go to pot. Just the opposite, right down to a light, baby powder and freesia scent.

Calvin didn't stand when his wife came in, and neither did Mrs. Almquist offer her ex-to-be any greeting.

Dunstan shot Jane a single, veiled glance: *Let the wild rumpus begin.*

Under the table, Jane toed off her ballet flats and prepared to model sweet reason and professional cooperation for the Almquists.

"Ms. DeLuca and I thought we'd use today's meeting to consider parenting schedules," Dunstan said, "but if we can't come up with something you both agree to, then Maryland law pretty much requires that you attempt mediation."

Calvin popped the latches on his briefcase. "You mean we have to pay for both? For you two spinning your wheels and then some touchy-feely counselor type wasting more of our time? Thanks so much. If we take long enough to figure out how I'm to become a stranger to my own children, then we won't have to worry about paying for their college educations, because I'll be too broke."

Doreen slapped both palms onto the table. "You're already a stranger to them, though they're *our* children. The point of this divorce is to ensure you become a stranger to me too. Nobody told you to go for the partner slot, Cal. That was your decision."

"Children cost money, Dorie."

Some attorneys would have let this venting and posturing go on until the clients ran out of steam, but Jane had already had enough.

"Your bickering costs money too, at least when Mr. Cromarty and I are in the room. You can stand out in the parking lot all afternoon berating each other, but today we're supposed to focus on your children. How are they doing?"

Playing the kid card so early was a calculated risk, but this time, it paid off. Husband and wife exchanged sad, guilty looks.

"Mark asked me if I was moving to DC," Calvin said. "He was giving me permission—my own son, *giving me permission*—to abandon him. Luke won't say anything, but…"

But a child's silences could bludgeon even an absent parent.

Dunstan pushed his glasses up his nose and passed over several pieces of paper. "Mrs. Almquist and I came up with this schedule for tax season, which we understand to be Mr. Almquist's busiest time. We're hoping that over the summer, the boys can spend more time with their father."

"So I get them when I'll have to take off work to look after them?" Calvin said, wrinkling his nose. "Or I can put them in hockey camp all summer, and forget about affording any vacations."

For the next hour, it went like that. Every attempt at concession from one spouse met with suspicion and grumbling from the other. One would indulge in a flare of temper while the other tried for compromise, then the roles would switch. Jane intervened when her own client was particularly nasty, Dunstan reined in Mrs. Almquist when she was similarly uncooperative.

Dunstan was inclined to roam the room, and at one point he cracked the conference room door a few inches for no reason Jane could discern, because the room was neither warm nor cold.

They eventually wrangled a basic schedule into place, though both parties would take the next week to consider the tentative agreement.

"I'll make copies of these," Dunstan said, collecting the most recent version of the four-week parenting pattern. "Doreen, if you'd join me for a moment?"

"What are they talking about?" Calvin asked, though the question had none of his previous snark. Putting down on paper the reality of a family splitting apart would wallop the snark out of anybody.

"If the parenting agreement flies, then the next step is usually the division of marital assets, but I have a question for you, Calvin."

"I'm apparently full of answers today. I've never seen Dorie so subdued."

And this bothered him, which was the price extracted from a man who *could* pay attention to his wife, but hadn't for too long.

"For many couples, the parenting aspect of the divorce is the worst part. Once they know they'll still be able to spend time with their children, they can pay attention to the rest of the agenda more easily. Any time you want to put the divorce on pause and try some counseling with Doreen, you let me know."

At some point, Calvin's international document courier briefcase had found its way to the floor. He set it back on the table now as if it were a cinder block, not an essentially empty box.

"Doreen would never go to counseling, and there's no easy part to ripping your life in two. We'll get through the money issues, but I don't see how we'll hang on to that house. Dorie loves that house, and the boys have friends all over the neighborhood."

"That was sort of what I wanted to ask you. Doreen takes good care of herself."

He rummaged in his briefcase. "She does—tennis, spin classes, yoga, zumba, swimming, massages, and that sort of thing. Always has and has insisted I do likewise. She's right. A lot of the guys at the office are not exactly fit—accounting is a sedentary profession—but Dorie says if we don't want the kids to sit around playing video games all day, we need to get off our duffs too."

"You should thank her for that." *In counseling.*

Calvin closed the briefcase, crossed his arms on top of it, and rested his forehead on his wrists. "Then she'll snap at me, tell me if I could listen to her about staying fit, then why not about anything else? I'll snap back that nobody wants to listen to constant bitching…" He heaved a sigh and straightened. "What did you want to ask?"

"How does she afford all that upkeep? She's sporting salon nails, salon hair, and that was a lovely outfit. The shoes were either very good Jimmy Choo knock-offs or the real deal, and her handbag—" Would have paid for several counseling sessions by itself.

"I don't know this Choo guy, but Doreen manages on what I put in the household account. I suppose that will change."

Everything would change, everything except the leaden feeling old Cal drove up and down the interstate with each day, and that would hang around all too faithfully.

"All of those classes and memberships cost money, Cal. I'll bet she has her hair done down in DC and shops for her clothes at least at White Flint. Mr. Choo doesn't get out this way much. Do you typically give Doreen jewelry for birthdays and Christmas?"

He gazed off into the middle distance, an emotionally overwhelmed and exhausted man trying to make his intellect function. "Not jewelry. Dorie buys that herself—she has better taste than I ever will. I'll send her flowers, or stuff that can be planted."

Dorie had been wearing four rings—in addition to her wedding rings, interestingly—each sporting a semi-precious stone in a craftsman setting, as well as bracelets and earrings to match.

"Her household account will bear some scrutiny," Jane said, discreetly toeing her right ballet flat back onto her foot. "Maybe she clips a lot of coupons, maybe she's a secret shopper, but nobody looks that well put together for nothing."

"She smells good too," Calvin said wistfully, now that nobody of any import could overhear him. "Even when she comes home from the gym, that woman smells good and has every day I've known her. The boys will have to do some looking to find wives who measure up to the standard Doreen has set."

Ah, the sentimentality of the soon-to-be single.

"Maintaining that standard when you're trying to establish a second household will be a challenge, Cal, and I can promise you Doreen will not meet that challenge graciously."

Jane maneuvered the left ballet flat on and stood. "I can send you the notes if you want to be on your way. The weather's supposed to get stinky this afternoon, and the temperature has already started to drop. You might want get going before the drizzle starts freezing. Mr. Cromarty and I will probably need some time to confer anyway."

"About?"

Calvin was not a trusting soul, but that was to be expected when his wife of seventeen years had turned into a stranger, and his children could well do likewise.

"Who's to draft the parenting agreement, when will he have Doreen's version of the financial statement together, when will I have yours? This stagecoach doesn't drive itself, but you're off to a good start."

Sort of like congratulating somebody on putting together an excellent funeral.

He checked his watch, a big, clunky, fourteen-function deal held to his wrist with the jeweler's equivalent of a chain-link fence. Nobody wore a watch any more, cell phones serving the need more than adequately, but Calvin probably relished the comfort of a dedicated timepiece that doubled as an altimeter and food processor.

"I'm off to the salt mines, then. At least this time of day, traffic will be light."

"You ever think of telecommuting one or two days a week in the off-season?"

Jane telecommuted frequently when she didn't have to be in court. Put on her best bathrobe and most comfy slippers, popped open her laptop, and alternated drafting legal motions with Spider Solitaire marathons all from the comfort of her favorite corner of the sofa.

Nothing like a seemingly impossible game of Spider for helping the subconscious tackle sticky legal puzzles.

"One of the partners telecommutes," Cal said, shrugging into a Burberry raincoat. "She lives on the other side of Baltimore. The gas and commuting time made the argument for her, though during tax season, it's all hands on deck, no matter where you live."

On that naval note, he departed for his rainy commute.

CHAPTER THREE

Anybody handling divorce work needed to acquaint themselves with the traditional phases of grieving: denial, anger, bargaining, depression, and acceptance. Clients ricocheted through them, sometimes touching four out of five in the space of ten minutes.

The fifth phase...acceptance. That one was elusive. Dunstan sensed the Almquists might never attain it.

"Don't look out the window," Jane DeLuca said, stuffing her undersized computer into her oversized carpetbag. "Our clients are not at their best."

"One doesn't expect them to be," Dunstan said, passing over copies of the first-round parenting schedule. He, of course, took a gander out the window so he could surreptitiously open it another three inches and begin detoxing the baby powder nerve gas from the room. "Oh, for God's sake."

"I warned you," Jane said, coming to stand beside him. "Pathetic, but predictable. I've tried to nudge Cal into counseling, but he's the white knuckle divorce type, apparently."

Under the old oak, dead leaves drifting around them, rain mizzling down, Calvin held Doreen and stroked her hair. Mrs. Almquist was clearly in tears, and Calvin...

"Your client is pretty broken up about this divorce," Dunstan said, knowing he should look away, but enjoying a moment with opposing counsel standing next to him, despite the sad tableau under the oak *and* the tickle in his sinuses. "Hit him by surprise."

And that wasn't what Dunstan had expected. Embezzlers were a canny lot, usually. The cheeriest people you'd ever want to meet, all the while sliding a hand into your pocket.

"They seem like a good team," Jane said. "I get that violent relationships need to end, but for people like these, I can't fathom what is so awful, what is so damned, unbearably miserable, that signing up for Match.com looks good in comparison to what you've spent years building with your children's other parent."

"One of life's great mysteries. My Uncle Donald says if birds can mate for life, great apes ought to be able to pull it off."

"What does your aunt say?"

"Uncle isna married." Though he had close and abiding relationships with his pocket flask and his weaponry.

"Dunstan, may I ask you something?"

And here it came, the sticky, tricky question, about foregoing court-ordered discovery on the financial documents, or about sending the clients for financial mediation, where such informality was often the norm.

"Aye, but let's move away from the window."

For the Almquists were having a good, long, miserable cuddle amid the dead leaves and autumn mist.

"I don't begrudge them a moment to console each other," Jane said, stuffing the schedule into the depths of her carpetbag. "But too much of that, and they'll turn their gun sights on us."

Because whatever animosity the divorce engendered often did end up being aimed at *the lawyers*, giving parties desperate for common ground targets they could both fire at.

"They'll get around to playing get-the-lawyers eventually anyhow," Dunstan said, closing the curtain over the window. Which was a…mistake. The day was dreary, and closing the curtains cast the small conference room into a cozy gloom, like a confessional. "If you're about to ask about waiving formal discovery, I haven't discussed the notion with my client."

Nor would he. Waiving formal discovery, where the court oversaw the fact-finding phase of the case, was ill-advised.

"Discovery shouldn't be a problem," Jane said, zipping her carpetbag closed. "I get the sense your client has control of all the household accounts and bills, so most of the documentation should come from her."

"You're shorter today. Shorter than usual." He liked that, though he also liked how she prowled around in her spiky heels, a family law superheroine in pursuit of any villains bent on world domination.

"I'm short every day." She plucked Dunstan's glasses from his nose and handed them to him. "Are these for show, or do you really need them? Glasses make a great courtroom prop. I wore flats because it's raining, or sleeting, or something."

She scooted onto the conference table and kicked out a foot with a slipper-looking black shoe on it.

Dunstan busied himself tidying papers into no particular order rather than examine her feet. He'd touched her ankle bones, found them slim and sharp, her calf sturdy, and—

He needed to get out more, and not to the Knightley brothers' poker nights.

"Sensible of you, I'm sure, to forego the heels. When do you expect to file your motions for discovery?"

"In the library the other day, and at the restaurant, did you touch my—touch *me* on purpose?"

The question was oh-so-casual and completely unexpected, as the best cross-examination could be. A world of possibilities lay in that question, most of them bad.

"If I say yes, you'll have me up before the bar association for sexual harassment, sent off to naughty-lawyer classes and begging to keep my license, or at the very least, you'll move to kick me off this case."

She might also charge him with assault for the hell of it, assault being any harmful or offensive touching. The state's attorney was a right bastard who'd delight in handling the case too.

No sense of humor at the prosecutor's office, though the first time, in the library, Dunstan hadn't entirely intended to take liberties.

And Dunstan hadn't earned nearly enough of the Almquist retainer. Then too, if Jane knew her client's hands were financially dirty, forcing Mrs. Almquist to change lawyers would obscure that difficult reality nicely.

A wonderful legal analysis of the facts, far too late to do him any good.

"James Knightley claims you meet some very nice people in naughty-lawyer classes," Jane said, scooting off the conference table. "Not that he's attended."

James Knightley was damned good-looking, also shrewd. He was the local expert on corporate law, which meant he could—and did—date the entire rest of the

Damson County Women's Bar Association with little chance of a conflict of interest.

"Let me ask you a question, then, Counselor," Dunstan said. He unhooked Jane's raincoat from the rack and held it open for her. "Was your wee foot trying to evade my hand? On either occasion?"

Because another hypothesis could explain why she'd bring this up now:

Jane DeLuca, spikey-heeled terror of the Damson County family law bar, needed to get out more too.

* * *

Dunstan Cromarty had the knack of holding a lady's coat so she didn't have to contort herself into it, but could instead stand more or less passively while her outerwear was slipped up her arms and draped over her shoulders.

The sensation was…lovely and novel, and that Jane allowed this courtesy probably answered any questions about her *wee fute* and whether she'd complain to the bar association about a moment or two of slap and tickle.

"Dunstan, where's your staff?" Jane asked, because she and opposing counsel were apparently to have a somewhat awkward conversation about boundaries and professionalism.

About which her feet were not happy at all.

"My staff is larking about Lancaster County on some quilt tour. They asked for the day off weeks ago, and I usually manage well enough without them. My paralegal's only half time, and my secretary leaves at three thirty to pick up her kids."

Knowing he was a good boss did nothing to help Jane maintain a professional distance. "Why aren't you in Scotland, Cromarty?"

"I often think of going home, but I won't do that until my coffers will allow a successful transition to practice there. When you're a solo practitioner, and all the overhead falls to you, you make little financial headway."

He said this standing behind Jane, as if he didn't want her to see him admit homesickness, or the weariness that came with being a solo practitioner.

"Tell me about it," Jane said, stepping away. She cracked the curtain over the window and saw the Almquists giving each other a final hug beside a blue SUV, Cal's briefcase at his feet, his hand braced near his wife's shoulder.

"Jane, about your question?"

She could tell by his tone that the awkward discussion would be blessedly brief. He'd meant nothing, he hadn't been flirting, it wouldn't happen again. No harm, no foul.

No more lunches without cutlery, no more speculating about what Dunstan Cromarty looked like wearing only his glasses.

"You have very pretty feet," he said, which was an interesting opening statement, but whatever else he might have said was lost in a great sneeze that he silenced by pinching his nose closed.

"Didn't your mother tell you not to do that?" Jane asked, shouldering her carpetbag. "You're supposed to let a sneeze out, not trap it, because it can do all kinds of—Dunstan? Cromarty?"

He stood bent forward a few peculiar inches at the waist, one hand braced on the conference table. His expression had a listening quality, like a juvenile delinquent who'd just knocked back a fifth of Jim Beam might listen for the approach of sirens—or death.

Jane set her bag on the table. "Dunstan, is something wrong? You've gone pale."

Even his lips were pale, and his eyes suggested his innocent client had just been given twenty to life.

"Are you having a heart attack?"

He eased out a breath. "Nay. Not a heart attack. It's m' back." He commenced to swearing softly, carefully, such as a man does when even breathing too deeply promises crippling pain.

Jane caught a few "fookin's," a "shite," and some other words that were too heavily accented for her to make out.

"Do we need to get you to urgent care?"

Because she was alone with him—drat and damn all quilt tours—and she couldn't leave him like this. Fortunately, she had neither court nor client appointments for the rest of the day, though she had work aplenty.

"I'll be fine. Some heat, some rest, a wee dram or two, and I'll come right. I always have before. You can run along now."

He hadn't moved, hadn't shifted his posture a single millimeter.

"*Run along*? And leave you the oil can? You won't be that lucky. I let you pay for lunch, you'll let me drive you home."

He wanted to argue. Jane could see the words fighting to get past his white lips, could see pride and pragmatism having a badass rumble, with common sense holding all bets.

"I'll get your briefcase," she said. "What else do you need?"

"I'll be—"

"You'll be laid up for a couple days, but if you tell me which files to grab, you can at least stare at them until the wee drams work their magic. If you argue with me on this, I'll tickle you."

"Shameless tactics," he muttered, as he began a slow, shuffling, half-bent progress toward the door. "The Almquist file will do. Throw in the Fosters' agreement too—that one's on my desk. Grab Baxter while you're about it, and maybe Ostergard, as well."

"You're taking a couple days at home, Dunstan, not setting up a home office. Where are your keys?"

Progress to the parking lot was slow and silent, with Jane carrying both her carpetbag and Dunstan's battered briefcase.

"I'll not be able to get out of that," Dunstan said as they approached Jane's powder-blue Prius. "And gettin' in won't be a treat, either."

While she sympathized with his misery, Jane had rather enjoyed his bad language. "What do you propose?"

"My vehicle will do."

His vehicle. The small parking lot held three other cars, all with a dusting of wet, yellow oak leaves and the occasional oversized snowflake. "The Camry?"

"The Tundra."

A Tundra was a…truck. A big, muddy black truck with the tailgate down and testosterone tires such as Jane could have neither lifted nor afforded. "You can get into that thing?"

"I'll haul myself up by the handles. You'll have to drive."

First, she had to wait as Dunstan by groans and inches shifted himself up into the passenger's seat. He settled back slowly, slowly, never seeming to reach a place of comfort. Jane slammed his door closed and came around to the driver's side.

Getting in was undignified, and the seat was way too far back, but the view was lovely.

"I've always wanted to drive a truck," she said, fitting the key into the ignition and cranking the engine. "I like sitting up this high, and these seats are cushy. Is this the seat heater?"

She hit two buttons, cranking his up to high and putting her own at medium. Everything on the dash was fairly self-explanatory, and the truck steered beautifully.

So it was completely by accident that Jane bumped a rear wheel over a curb pulling out, causing Dunstan to curse for nearly half a block in a language she didn't recognize.

* * *

Please, Almighty Merciful God, do not let Wallace be playing turd hockey on the kitchen floor when I hobble in the door with Jane DeLuca at my side.

"You haven't passed out on me, have you?" Jane asked as she shut the truck off. "Your eyes are closed."

"I'm gathering my strength." For any number of ordeals.

"Don't you move until I've rappelled down the cliff side," she said, scrambling out of the driver's seat.

She was so little, she had to more or less jump out of the truck, while Dunstan... He moved one leg, then the other. He paused to let the agony bounce around in his body, then used the handles to haul himself sideways, and so it went, one indignity, one torment at a time.

Jane shouldered their various bags, while Dunstan caught sight of Wallace sitting in the living room window, a marmalade ball of gloating feline.

"Oh, you have a kitty! What's his name?"

"Fat Bastard. The door's nae locked."

She opened the door and stood back so Dunstan could totter past her, then she hauled their bags in and closed the door. "Is an unlocked door prudent? You're fairly isolated here."

"I'm hoping somebody will come by and steal the cat." Who, in an unprecedented display of survival instinct, had neither recently used the litter box, nor undertaken any hockey games that Dunstan could see.

It being a hallmark of Wallace's hockey seasons that cat litter was sprinkled from one end of the downstairs to the other.

"I love these old farm houses," Jane said, shrugging out of her coat. "They have charm."

Dunstan stretched out a casual hand and braced himself against the nearest wall, a compromise between his tattered dignity and the urge to crumple in a screaming fetal heap three steps inside the door.

"These old farm houses have heating bills. If you'd like to take my truck back to town, I can have one of the Knightleys give me a lift tomorrow."

He didn't attempt a smile, neither did he try to get to the sofa, a good five yards, three cursing fits, and four prayers off across the living room. Carpeted yards, though, which would make crawling ever so much more comfy.

"I'm not going anywhere," Jane said, and damn the woman, she spoke with the patient amusement of a small female with a perfectly functional sacroiliac. "The first order of business should be to get you into a hot shower, if your bad back is anything like my grandpa's. Is your bedroom upstairs?"

"I'll be adorning the sofa for a wee bit before attempting anything so ambitious as a shower." Though a shower…His muscles stopped pounding on his tailbone long enough to beg for that hot shower even before he opened his last bottle of twenty-five-year-old Glenmorangie single malt.

"So you can't make it up the stairs. Does this level have a bathroom?"

He didn't like this line of questioning one bit. "Aye."

"Then what are you waiting for?"

Disaster for Scotland, to put the situation mildly. "I'm waiting for the floor to open up and swallow me whole. I'll not allow you to undress me, Jane DeLuca."

Not like this, please God. Not like this.

"So we'll put you in the shower with your clothes on. Would you leave me to suffer when my back hurt so badly I couldn't stand the thought of sneezing again?"

He crossed himself with the hand that wasn't anchored to the wall. "You're a cruel woman to mention such a thing. There'll be no sneezing of any kind for the foreseeable future."

And not to put too fine a point on it, his diet would be rich in fiber, once he could stand in the kitchen long enough to pour milk on cereal. Wallace chose then to strop himself across Dunstan's legs.

"He knows I canna kick him."

Jane inserted herself under Dunstan's outstretched arm, which was about three seconds away from shaking. "Lean on me. Anybody who names a cat Fat Bastard has already abused the animal. I assume the facilities are down the hall?"

Miles away, of course. Why didn't old farm houses have bathrooms in the foyer?

"Second door on the left."

He tried not to lean on her—and failed. Jane was surprisingly sturdy, though, and they covered the distance to the bathroom with only a bit more swearing. Then she abandoned him—abandoned him—with an admonition to get off as much of his clothing as he could while she retrieved sweats from his bedroom upstairs.

Sometimes, when his back went out, within twenty minutes, he could tell he was due for only a light penance. A dose of painkiller, time lying prone, a movie or two, and all could be forgiven, provided he took no chances for several days.

This was shaping up to be a less accommodating episode.

Dunstan undressed in the bathroom, his clothes piled into a heap at his feet, for he could not bend down to hang them up and couldn't balance on one foot long enough to hook them with his toes—he knew all the tricks. He could manage to brush his teeth and tend to other standing rituals, and by the time he heard a tap on the door, he was sporting only a towel about his hips.

"It's nae locked."

"Good," Jane said, pushing the door closed behind her. "I found sweats, but wouldn't a kilt be easier? You don't have to step into it."

She brandished a black work kilt Dunstan wore when waging his endless war with the yard.

"That's a fetching ensemble you're wearing yourself, Ms. DeLuca." For she'd changed into gray sweats and a green T-shirt that said *If it takes three years to get there, it had better be one helluva bar.*

"I always have gym clothes with me," she said, turning on the bathtub taps and holding her hand under the gushing stream.

Maybe she frequently found herself sleeping in places other than her own bed? Not a cheering thought.

She fiddled with the taps, and soon, water streamed from the shower head in steamy abundance. The difficulty before Dunstan daunted him: He had to raise each foot high enough to step into the shower and shift his weight without falling.

"In you go," Jane said, showing no indication of absenting herself. "If you think I'll let you risk a slip-and-fall now, you're dumber than I thought." She stepped closer and put her arms around Dunstan's bare torso. "Lean on me, and no heroic measures, because I'll probably topple with you, and I will sue you if I injure anything other than my pride."

He leaned, he tottered, he leaned some more, and finally, finally, found his way to the soothing, hot spray. Jane whisked his towel off and flipped the Royal Stewart plaid shower curtain closed in the same nanosecond, but the bliss of the hot water was so great, Dunstan almost didn't care what she saw, or what she thought of what she saw.

Almost.

* * *

Jane hadn't looked, truly she hadn't, but she'd *seen* anyway.

She paused outside the bathroom door, back braced against the wall as images of a naked Dunstan Cromarty danced through her head—and a few points south.

A long, tapered back that flowed into a taut, male tush; defined musculature on every limb; the proverbial washboard abs; and a chest that really deserved to be immortalized on the covers of a few romance novels.

And as for the rest...

She contemplated the rest of him, *at length*, as it were, until the shower stopped. In the ensuing silence, reason rescued Jane from considering career suicide: Dunstan Cromarty wasn't interested in her. That's what his *pretty fute* speech would have been about, had he been allowed to finish it.

"Do not even think of getting out of that shower, Dunstan Cromarty," Jane called, as she opened the bathroom door. Fragrant steam beclouded her senses, along with the knowledge that a big, wet, hurting Scot stood on the other side of the shower curtain.

"Pass me the towel, Jane, or I'll scandalize us both."

Let the scandalizing begin. "This one's dry." She slid a fluffy red bath towel around the end of the shower curtain. "Towel off as best you can, and then I'll pass you the kilt."

He didn't manscape. He probably didn't even know what manscaping was, and Jane hoped he never learned.

"I'll have that kilt now."

The damp towel was thrust forth. Jane made the swap. "Do you feel any better?"

"Aye, a bit. I'll break out the heating pad, take a few pills, and settle in for the rest of the day. This will pass."

Jane leaned against the wall, trying not to picture Dunstan Cromarty fastening on a kilt. "Do you have court tomorrow?"

"Nay, thank Christ. I wouldna answer for the consequences if I had to listen to Elvin Gregory's bleating when my back's troubling me. No court until next week. You?"

"Same. Shall we get you out of there?"

The shower curtain whipped back, revealing a damp Dunstan Cromarty wearing nothing but a pleated black kilt and a scowl. "I can manage."

"I can help." He hated this, hated being seen helpless, and Jane could understand that. "My Aunt Della fell in the shower and busted a hip. She lay there for more than a day before my cousin found her."

A heavy arm settled across Jane's shoulders. "You're such a ray of sunshine, wee Jane. How have I functioned without you in my bathroom all these years? In case you haven't noticed, I'm not your auld auntie."

"One foot at a time," Jane said, tucking an arm around his waist.

He moved somewhat more easily, so Jane let him find his way to the couch on his own and tidied up in the bathroom. She left the door open to let the steam out, tossed the dirties and the used towels in a closet washing machine and started the load.

"Where's the heating pad?"

"In the linen closet upstairs, but you mustn't let the cat see you plugging it in."

"I noticed cat food in a plastic container labeled 'Wallace.' Do you have more than one cat?"

Dunstan eased back on the sofa cushions, and carefully, carefully, stretched out full length. "His proper name is Fat Bastard Wallace Cromarty. The whiskey's above the cat food in the pantry. Perhaps you'll share a dram with me?"

The Scots were reputed to be a hospitable lot, unless they were planning murder or treason—much like the Italians. Jane went off in search of hooch and a heating pad.

Dunstan's house was tidy, even his king-size bed was made—cozy Black Watch plaid flannel sheets and wool blankets—and his personal bathroom was spotless. Sheets and towels in the linen closet were neatly folded and stacked, lavender soaps and sachets tucked between them.

And yet, two spare rooms down the hall from his bedroom were empty. Not sparsely furnished, but echoingly empty. No curtains, no stacked boxes.

The pantry shelves presented the same picture: What stores Dunstan had—healthy cereal, canned soup (low salt, not low fat), tea, coffee, a bag of gourmet bite-size dark chocolates—were arranged for easy access, but more than half the shelves were empty.

And only one box of pasta, one can of tomato sauce, one can of chili beans, though again, the quality was good.

"Why do you stock your larder like an old person?" Jane asked as she plugged in the heating pad.

"Now you've done it. Wallace and that heating pad have an unnatural relationship."

The heating pad's flannel sleeve was Black Watch plaid. Wallace hopped down from the upright piano and positioned himself sphinx-like on the arm of the sofa.

"He heard you summon him," Jane said, though the cat's dimensions suggested an open can of fancy white albacore was the only summons he truly heeded. "Scoot a bit."

Dunstan snatched the heating pad from her rather than allow her to tuck it behind him. "I'll do it."

He positioned it low against his back—very low.

"You have two empty rooms upstairs," Jane said. "Is that Scottish frugality, or a sign of impending departure for the Auld Sod?"

Because somewhere in the *Lonely Woman's Handbook of Heartbreak*, it was written that just as that woman finally found a man who might—*might*—interest her, he had to ship out for his next assignment, transfer to the home office, or otherwise become geographically compromised.

Though Jane was not interested in Dunstan Cromarty, Esquire. *Could not* be interested in him.

He closed his eyes, and rather than stand over him, Jane took a seat on the carpeted floor, which created a curious, eye-level intimacy.

"I'll go home, eventually," he said. "My mother claims she lives for the day, though she's little ones aplenty and all three of my siblings to console her. I'm in practice by myself. All the revenue is mine and all the bills too. You know what that's like."

He had done a better job than Jane had at creating a home. His piano had pictures of *people* on it; family, judging from the number of big, smiling men in kilts. The mantel over the woodstove held framed awards and more pictures, one of them a panoramic photograph of some gray stone castle by a beautiful, still lake.

"Take these," Jane said, passing him two pills. "I found them upstairs. I'm guessing you bought them in the UK, because they have codeine in them and they're not prescription."

"That I did." He downed the pills. "I forgot I had them in my luggage, which doesn't say much for the constabulary in Customs."

A sip of water came next, a tricky undertaking when supine. Jane resisted the urge to support Dunstan's head and took the glass back when he'd finished.

"I've been in Damson County for five years," she said, stroking a hand over Wallace's thick fur, "and I still have boxes of stuff I moved up here from DC. I've thought about switching apartments after the first of the year, but then I'd be committing the mortal sin of moving the same boxes twice."

Dunstan turned his head to offer her a small, conspiratorial smile.

"My boxes are in the garage. I should be in practice with a partner, of course. When I set up shop, I was the new fellow, and I talked funny. Still do, but a partner reduces the risks. You have a partner."

"Not any more. Louise chucked all the glamour and glory of small town legal practice for art school and a certain art professor. Now I have an office big enough for two lawyers and nobody to gripe about it to."

"Gripe to me. I'm a captive audience, and I'm developing an unnatural relationship with the couch and the heating pad both. Wallace has set me a bad example, you see. You, fortunately, are putting my cat to sleep, or he'd be tormenting me in my helpless and vulnerable state."

For all his grousing about the cat, Dunstan was less uncomfortable. Jane deduced this from his eyes, from his color, from the way he relaxed into the sofa cushions. And Wallace wasn't going to sleep. He wouldn't when he was on duty as a guardian kitty of Clan Cromarty's Maryland branch.

"I miss Louise." Jane scratched Wallace's white bib of a chin rather than admit she hadn't meant to say that. "She would come slamming back from court, ranting about Judge Mansfield's bias against people named Horatio, or the prosecutor's inability to organize a docket, and I could come back with lazy opposing counsel and cheating spouses."

"I hate it when they cheat, though I don't blame them. Loneliness is the most dangerous and sincere precursor to stupidity."

He stuffed a pillow under his head, making the muscles of his chest flex, and Jane endured a bolt of sincerity passing right down her middle.

"I can't blame the ones who cheat," Jane said, "but if you'll cheat on your spouse, you'll cheat on your cheat. What sort of foundation is that to move forward on?"

They fell silent while Wallace set up a stentorian purring, co-counsel in agreement with any discussion that kept people close enough to pet him. The cat's expression was knowing and smug, even for a very large, well loved cat.

Insight popped into Jane's mind like Gopher popping up in the middle of the night to visit One Stuck Bear.

Doreen Almquist was cheating.

All of that polish and shine, the time at the gym, the designer wardrobe, the perfect hair, wasn't for the husband she never saw. It was to impress the personal trainer, the sugar daddy—

The guy who bought her all of that jewelry and the fancy perfume.

"You look angry, wee Jane. Is it time for you to leave? Wallace might appreciate a bit of tucker in his dish before you go."

He wouldn't ask for himself, but he'd ask for a cat large enough to have its own gravitational field.

"Family law can be such a trial."

"Put that on a T-shirt, why don't you? Every family law practitioner on the planet would buy it in three different colors."

"I'm abandoning you," Jane said, rising. "Wallace, keep an eye on the patient. I'll be in the kitchen addressing the sore lack of decent victuals on these premises. Dunstan, do you need anything? Once I start cooking, I'm hard to interrupt."

"My files."

"Hopeless," Jane said, though if he could focus on work, then his back was doing better.

Which meant cooking was simply an excuse to stay here, in the half-empty home of a guy Jane could ethically share a professional friendship with—but no more.

* * *

Wallace at least waited until Jane had disappeared into the kitchen to march across Dunstan's chest and settle on his belly.

"She likes you," Dunstan said. Then more quietly, "I like her."

He reached—carefully—for the Almquist file, then set it aside in favor of the Baxter guardianship, a more or less uncontested matter. Wallace had positioned himself so Dunstan could hold a file too close to read easily or too far away.

"Damned cat."

The Baxter order was well drafted—Trenton Knightley knew what he was about—and the Ostergard pleadings were ready to submit.

Outside, the wind had picked up, and if Dunstan hadn't been nursing his back, he would have loaded up the woodstove. Instead, he pulled the tartan blanket off the back of the couch, suffering Wallace's back claws to his belly for his trouble, only to have the cat re-establish residency when Dunstan had twitched and tugged the blanket into place.

The painkillers were taking effect, subduing the ache in Dunstan's back, while an ache of a different sort rose up in its place.

He subdued that ache with his notes from the Almquists' meeting.

"Something tasty this way comes," Dunstan informed the cat some time later. "Though I don't know what Jane found to cook up. If you were any sort of friend, you'd go on reconnaissance instead of using me for your personal chafing dish."

Jane emerged from the kitchen, a wooden spoon in her hand. "Are you on the phone?"

"Arguing with my cat," Dunstan said, feeling foolish. She'd called his pantry elderly, and old people also talked to their cats. "And winning."

"Ha. Try this." She knelt and held the spoon up to Dunstan's mouth. He took a nibble of tomato, oregano, a hint of cilantro, heat, cumin…

"Does it need something? I like a little heat, a little spice, a hint of sweetness…bold, but not pushy." She tasted from the same spoon Dunstan had, and innuendo blended with the spices, at least in Dunstan's male mind. An image of Jane wearing nothing but her spike heels and a smile—heat, spice, sweetness, and boldness—assaulted him.

"Go for bold," Dunstan said. "The sauce has to stand up to the meat."

"Right. Bold is good. Do you need your glasses?"

He needed a cold shower, which might do permanent damage to his back.

"Aye. Yonder paperweight means I can't view anything from a proper distance." In more ways than one.

"You, come with me." Jane scooped the cat from Dunstan's lap, her hand brushing low across his belly through the blankets. "Leave your buddy in peace so he can deal with his lawyer guilt."

Wallace turned his best take-me-to-your-tuna-fish stare on Jane, while Dunstan put the Ostergard file on his lap. "He's not allowed on the counter."

"Oh, right. All day when you're gone, he sits around staring heavenward, reciting the commandment about not hopping up on spotless counters. He has you so trained."

They disappeared into the kitchen, Jane muttering about stubborn males, Wallace doing his impersonation of a besotted rag doll.

While Dunstan stared at a file that, even with his glasses on, in his present condition, he had little chance of reading.

CHAPTER FOUR

"You must be feeling better," Jane said, though *better* was a relative term. Dunstan had moved from the couch far enough to heed nature's call, and he'd downed a gratifying quantity of chili, but he'd eaten his supper on the couch, a blanket around his shoulders, heating pad at the ready, rather than sitting on a hard kitchen chair.

"I'll manage from here," Dunstan said, jamming a pillow behind his back. "Now it's mostly waiting for the ache to recede while I move about like an old man with a bad hangover."

"You won't overdo?"

"Oh, likely I will, but I've more of those magic pills and your magic chili. You're welcome to take the cat as a sign of my gratitude."

Wallace now sat tucked against Dunstan's side, feline Laird of the Western Couch.

"You can make it up the stairs?"

"That might be a challenge."

Something nagged at Jane, something besides the wish that she could, like a girlfriend, for example, spend the night fussing over him.

In the big bed with the cozy flannel sheets.

"Your house is cold, Dunstan. The kitchen was toasty because I cooked there, but here and up in the bedroom, you need some heat."

Which observation came out all wrong, factual though it was.

"I haven't serviced the furnace yet this year. The woodstove is normally all I need." He shifted and pushed and came to his feet, looking quite...quite tall wearing nothing but a kilt.

And not at all cold.

"Run along now, Jane. I'll survive."

Run along? Were he not ailing, she would have smacked him for that.

"Show me how to fire this thing up," Jane said, crossing to the squat, black iron stove in the fireplace. "It can't be that difficult."

"It's easy, if you've split enough of the wood that's been seasoning in the garage, which neither I nor Wallace have got 'round to yet."

Dunstan was trying to get rid of her, and that was smart. Then too, wearing only his kilt, he didn't seem affected by the chill seeping into Jane's bones.

"I'm supposed to leave you here, barely able to stand, your house freezing, with no one but that cat to look after you?"

"My back is much better, and by morning I'll be right enough. My bed is cozy, and the roads will only get messier the longer you tarry. Wet leaves can be slicker than ice, even if you have four-wheel drive. Away with you."

Pathetic, that he'd have to shoo her off so determinedly, and yet, Jane could see that even standing upright was costing him.

"The chili's in the fridge," Jane said, taking her coat from the chair she'd tossed it over hours ago. "I fed Wallace some of the Italian sausage when I was cooking, and the corn bread is in the pantry near the whiskey. We never did share that wee dram."

Not that she was about to drink it now, when dark, wet country roads awaited her.

And a cold apartment without so much as a healthy ficus plant to welcome her.

"My thanks, then," Dunstan said, walking with her to the door. "You're a good cook, Jane DeLuca, but don't worry. Your secret is safe with me."

"And you love your cat," she said, because it was as close to banter as she could dredge up. She found his keys in her coat pocket, shouldered her bag, and prepared to offer him a cheery farewell.

While to herself, she could admit she *liked* this guy. More than liked him, she respected him. How long had it been since a man, any man, had caught her eye? And worse, Dunstan Cromarty, with his cranky devotion to his cat, his Gaelic cussing, and his lonely frugality, caught her by the heart too, and that was—

That was rottenly unfair.

"My thanks," he said again, and while Jane had been silently railing at the universe, Dunstan had moved closer. He still smelled good, of his usual fragrance and some minty muscle rub he'd sneaked onto himself while Jane had done the dishes.

And now, shake hands? Thumbs up with a parting wink? Jaunty salute?

Jane was in her flats, so she had to brace a hand on Dunstan's chest to lean up and kiss his cheek. He held still for it, for the entire, lingering, humiliating, delightful duration of a presuming but not-quite-out-of-bounds parting kiss between friendly associates, and then his arms settled around her.

"If not for you, I'd be stretched out on the floor of my office praying for a coma by now," he muttered. "You're a managing female, and I'm grateful for it. Wallace says the same, and he doesn't give compliments lightly."

Jane's cheek rested against a bare, warm chest, a small fortification against a long, cold, lonely drive home. Jane was further consoled by the notion that nothing she had done with Dunstan, nothing *they* had done, would make facing each other across the conference table or the courtroom any more difficult.

Wonderfully professional of her, all this good behavior.

"I should be going." Dunstan should be letting her go, too.

His cheek came to rest against her hair. "Jane?"

"Hmm?" *Do not kiss this man. Do not lick this man. If you must breathe this man in, do so quietly.*

"The Almquist case calls for full discovery. Proper motions with the court, deadlines, interrogatories, depositions, the whole bit."

Was he *warning* her that his client had colored outside the lines? If so, what warning did she owe him? He wouldn't drop a dime on his own client, which meant he was warning Jane that it really was time for her to leave.

Which it was. Jane stepped back and didn't bother attempting any cheery bullshit, the loss of Dunstan's embrace being about the least cheery misery to befall her since she'd seen a two-time domestic assaulter walk off with custody of his three small children in her first year of practice.

"Full discovery makes sense," she said, though it would drag the case out for months, and the last thing she wanted to deal with any longer than necessary was this *situation* with Dunstan. "Sleep well."

She didn't offer to fetch him anything he might need from the office tomorrow. Let the ever gallant and resourceful Knightley pests perform that chore. Jane had an exceptionally thorough discovery order to draft, nosy interrogatories to pull together, hellacious depositions to plan—

"G'night, then, Jane. Drive carefully and use the seat heater."

He kissed her cheek and winked at her, the barbarian.

Jane opened the door, a blast of frigid, chilly air smacking her in the face. The day had been autumnal. The night—as predicted—had turned wintry.

Behind her, Dunstan began that soft, semi-Gaelic swearing she'd heard from him earlier in the day.

"That's ice coming down out there," he said, tugging Jane back from the door. "It's damned pouring ice, and you're not going anywhere."

* * *

Western Maryland enjoyed what Uncle Donald would have called Fickle Bitch weather. A November day could be seventeen degrees or seventy degrees, same with February. Whatever plans Dunstan made—to split wood over the coming weekend, for example—the weather could be relied upon to thwart them. After two weeks of Saint Martin's summer—Indian summer, *in American*—winter had apparently descended.

"Sometimes it only starts out with ice then changes back to rain," Jane said, clutching her carpetbag to her chest. "If they've salted the roads, it's probably still safe to drive."

Retreat on her part was smart, because circumstances had conspired to inflict on Dunstan an appreciation for opposing counsel that had only partly to do with her nimble legal mind.

"We'll give it an hour, then, but let's turn on the telly and see what the weather boys and girls have to say. If this is the first storm of the season, they'll be all over it."

"Should we turn on the heat first?"

"Aye, we should, but some frugal Scot hasn't had oil delivered yet this season, and I ran my furnace nigh dry last spring."

March, to be exact, because wood was cleaner and cheaper than oil, and Dunstan enjoyed slamming an ax down on a length of cured oak more than he enjoyed paying the oil bill. A lot more.

She set her bag down, but did not take off her coat. By the time they'd found a weather report, Dunstan was sharing a blanket with Jane on the sofa, Wallace wedged between them like a feline bundling board.

"Ice storms are so pretty," Jane said more than an hour later, "but I hate them. You can't go anywhere, you can't shovel it off, you can't do anything but wait for it to melt and hope the power stays on."

Though for the duration of some movie Dunstan couldn't follow about a hooker falling in love with a young, well-dressed version of Richard Gere, you could cuddle on the couch with a woman who tempted you to highly unprofessional behavior.

You could take more pain medication. You could eat a second helping of very good chili.

"I've only the one bed, Jane, but it has a mattress warmer. You'll be cozy up there."

Or you could argue with a woman half your size and twice your fight about where to sleep.

"You need a decent night's sleep, Dunstan. I can curl up here with Wallace."

He reasoned, he taunted, he considered getting her drunk, but in his present condition. he couldn't carry her up the steps anyway, so he did what few Scots had ever learned to do well, he retreated.

She was gracious, agreeing to keep the heating pad with her. She pulled a pink plastic bag from her Mary Poppins satchel and disappeared into the bathroom.

Being only a fool rather than a very great fool, Dunstan used her absence to totter up the stairs, though he could feel Wallace's smirk with each careful, uneven step.

Wallace was likely overcome by hilarity when, around one in the morning, Dunstan woke to realize the power was out. His bed was delightfully cozy, but the battery backup on his digital alarm clock was blinking madly, the mattress warmer had cut off, and the house was swaddled in a profound silence that suggested not even the fridge was running.

Jane would manage—she had Wallace, she had a wool blanket. She'd curled up in her coat, too.

By one thirty a.m., when Dunstan got up to use the facilities, those arguments weren't keeping him warm, much less the lady he found shifting restlessly on his couch.

"Come up to bed, Jane. You'll catch your death down here."

"You sh-should not have come down those stairs in the dark, Dunstan Cromarty. The EMTs are likely overwhelmed with calls tonight, and I'll be fine as long as Wallace—"

The cat hopped off the couch and strutted, tail up, for the kitchen.

"Come to bed," Dunstan said, extending a hand down to her. "I canna sleep thinking you're shivering away in my own house, while I'm warm and toasty between my flannel sheets."

She pushed the blanket aside and rose, though Dunstan did not flatter himself she cared for his tender sensibilities. The lady was enamored of his Black Watch plaid flannel sheets, lest there be any mistaking the matter.

He used his cell phone as a flashlight as he herded Jane up the stairs, then switched it off, because a bad storm could kill the power for days.

Jane draped her coat over his reading chair and dove under the covers.

"Cromarty, you are an honest man. This bed is h-heaven."

Heaven for her, hell for him. "Move over. You're on my side."

"Use the other side. I'm calling dibs on this one until spring thaw."

Arguing was what lawyers did. It was also what lovers did. Dunstan climbed in on the far side, the cool bedding providing no distraction whatsoever from his bedmate.

She shivered, which made the bed tremble, and created a dilemma for Dunstan having moral, ethical, pragmatic, erotic, and even—he *was* an honest man—romantic implications.

Which he would consider when the electricity came back on, or while waiting tables at some dive in Edinburgh, the sure fate of those disbarred for gross misconduct.

"Come here, wee Jane. You'll keep me awake with your shivering, and I need my beauty sleep."

He also needed his license to practice law, though it would not keep him warm under these covers. Neither would Jane's license perform that function for her.

"You come here," she said. "The feeling has come back in my feet, and I'm not budging."

He rolled to his side, tucked her against his chest, and wondered how many other former members of the bar had mentally practiced the question, *May I supersize that for you?*

* * *

Dunstan was warm, he smelled good, and he was warm. Any two of the three would have sufficed to send Jane's scruples out into the icy, blustery night. She scooted around to face him, bundled into his chest, and hiked her legs over his hips. Dunstan brought his thighs up under her backside and wrapped an arm around her middle, and everywhere, he was *warm*.

"Try to relax," he said. "Relax in your middle. You'll stop shivering sooner."

"Where's Wallace when you need him?"

"The bedroom door's open, and heat rises, so this is probably the least cold room in the house. He'll be upon us soon, literally."

A madness was upon Jane, a madness to exercise awful judgment with Dunstan Cromarty at least three times before morning. She wouldn't jeopardize her license to practice for anything less than a hat trick.

"Dunstan?"

"Go to sleep, Jane."

As if. "Even Wallace ignores you when you give orders like that. You're becoming aroused." With reassuring speed, too.

"I'm also over the age of thirty, and thus not at the mercy of my biology." He sounded amused, while he felt…

"I wouldn't mind being at the mercy of your biology."

A considering sort of silence ensued, while Jane's teeth stopped chattering and Dunstan's embrace became less utilitarian.

"You'd mind if we crossed that line, Jane. When we're in court, the Almquists snarling at each other, the accusations flying, the judge fed up with the lot of us, you'd mind that I knew exactly how your breasts felt in my hands. You wouldn't want me knowing the taste of you, and you'd hate that you knew the taste of me, or the feel of me as I—go to sleep."

Until that moment, Jane might have been content with a rousing argument, a lecture about professional integrity and circumstances conspiring, but Dunstan's burr rumbling through the darkness, his scent, his heat, put images in her head of intimacy and pleasure.

"I'll get out of the case," she said, kissing his chest. Of course, she'd get out of the case—easiest thing in the world to file a motion to strike her appearance and enter somebody else's.

Anybody else's.

Dunstan's hand landed in her hair, cradling her closer. "You need the money. So do I."

"No, we don't need it. We just want it. People get divorced every thirty seconds in this country. I haven't wanted to be intimate with a man for—"

He kissed her cheek. "Hush, woman. Please, God, hush."

"—years, and you're in worse shape than I am," Jane went on, this time kissing his throat. "You hush, and—"

His hand, big and warm, palmed her breast through her old T-shirt. "I'll get out of the case, too, if you'll only for the love of Almighty—"

She got her mouth on his, and while his body was warm, his mouth was *hot*. Blessedly, desperately hot.

Dunstan tried to draw back for about two seconds, but then Jane felt the instant when his professionalism lost the case entirely to the logic of loneliness and desire. He shifted so she was half-tucked under him, and his weight was the most delightful reassurance that Jane would stay warm through the night.

His tongue was a wonder on cross-examination, feinting, teasing, daring—

"Clothes," Jane managed. He drew back enough that she could get out of her sweats and T-shirt without gelding him or giving him a black eye, though it was a near thing on both counts.

"Take off my kilt," he said.

"You take it—" What the hell, *of course* she'd take his kilt off. She found the buckles and wrenched them loose. Then she found *him*.

"Careful," he whispered, "or this exercise in confused priorities will be over before it starts."

"Will not," Jane said, stroking her fingers down the hard, silky length of him. But having made the decision to be intimate with Dunstan, her sense of urgency abated, leaving her curiously bereft.

How long had it been since she'd reciprocated a man's desire for her? Since she'd felt that lovely contrast, between the soft underside of her breast and the callused tenderness of a male palm?

Was this what family law had done to her? Made her avoid the very relationships that could give life meaning?

"Where did you go, Jane?" Dunstan asked, his hand shaping breast.

"I'm here," she said, cradling his check against her palm. "Why did we become lawyers, Dunstan?"

He should have laughed at the question, for it was no kind of pillow talk. Instead, he offered the first year law student's answer. "To do good while doing well?"

She thought of Doreen Almquist's perfect hair and her bewildered ex-to-be holding her as she cried in a cold, wet parking lot.

"Are we doing either?"

"On a good day, I hope. I'll tell you a secret," he said, nuzzling her neck. "I'm no damned good at math, and I like to argue. That's why I'm a lawyer."

"That was why you went to law school, but it's not why you're a good lawyer."

From the jumbled heap of arousal, self-doubt, and career puzzlement, Jane extracted a truth:

She liked, respected, and was attracted to Dunstan Cromarty, and with good reason. He was a singularly worthy man. Giving up a case that wasn't likely to go well was no price to pay for exploring where that attraction might lead.

Getting into bed with him was the smartest move she'd made in years.

"You don't want to be in bed with the lawyer, good or otherwise," Dunstan said, tracing his finger over her lips. "And neither do I, so could we please dispense with the questioning?"

She bit his finger, gently, because he'd said *please*. "I want this to matter, Dunstan, and I want to savor it. I want it hot and slow, and—"

"And I want *you*." He eased his finger over her lips. "*Now*. Reach into the top drawer and find us a Frenchie."

"I'm on the pill, and I don't even know what a Frenchie—"

He cut off whatever closing arguments she might have appended with a slow, deep, wet kiss that made Jane's insides sing something other than *Auld Lang Syne*. She kissed him back, climbed over him, and prepared to argue with him about who would be on top of whom.

The first time.

"Dunstan, are you comfortable on your back?"

"Aye, except for a wee ache in m' goolies."

"What are—?"

He nudged up. *Those* goolies.

"I ache too, and I don't even have goolies," she said, scraping her nails over his nipples.

"We'll let that be our secret. For much of the male bar association would have it otherwise when they oppose you."

He trapped her hands, and the moment became serious. The air Jane breathed was cold, probably cold enough that she could see her breath, but the entire house was in darkness. The clicky-wet sound of ice hitting the windows underscored the sense that beneath the covers, with Dunstan, was the only heat Jane would find anywhere.

"Love me," she whispered, right against his lips.

Dunstan Cromarty went about his loving the way he prosecuted his cases— thoroughly, with attention to detail, nothing sloppy or haphazard. When Jane might have rushed through their initial coupling, he slowed her down, with naughty whispers, soft caresses, and a patient, almost stealthy joining of their bodies.

"You feel,"—Jane cast around for a word to capture the way he filled her up, inexorably, sweetly, powerfully, completely—"*sublime*. If you don't let me catch my breath, I'll come, Dunstan."

He didn't let her catch her breath. Not the first time, or the second. By the third, though, Jane had found that Dunstan Cromarty had sensitive earlobes— something nobody had bothered to discover with him previously—and she could drive him to distraction with just her mouth.

"You have much to answer for," Dunstan whispered. "Taking advantage of my delicate back, driving me 'round the bend with your naughty mouth. The time has come for you to pay, Jane DeLuca."

He was strong, and determined, and because Jane was on top, Dunstan's hands were free to torment her, and torment her, he did. He worked his thumb between them and applied a steady pressure to a part of Jane already gone screamingly sensitive.

And if this was Dunstan with a delicate back…

"Damn you," Jane panted when pleasure blossomed, hot and relentlesse, once again. "You too, Dunstan."

With her last shred of strategy, she took his earlobe between her finger and thumb and pinched hard and that, ah yes, *that*.

"Yes. Yes, *yes*, Dunstan Lachlan Cromarty—"

He covered her mouth with his, while bliss shimmered through Jane, brighter, longer, more than she could endure, and yet, endure it she did, for Dunstan endured it with her.

She would have pitched off him immediately, the better to breathe and reactivate her brain, but Dunstan's embrace prevented it.

"Give me a minute," he said. "Please. Tissues are on the night table."

She would give him years, if he were inclined to take them. "Your back's okay?"

"Bugger my back. My earlobes will glow for a week."

He sounded pleased, and his hand drifting over Jane's back was so tender that tears threatened. She snuggled closer. "If I had goolies, they'd glow for a month."

He kissed her temple, and Jane remained snuggled to his chest, fighting sleep and tears both, because she did have a heart, and as delicate as extricating herself from the Almquist case would be, trying to disentangle herself from the man sharing the bed with her would be impossible.

* * *

"He won't let me out."

Jane sounded panicked, though her panic was controlled.

Dunstan closed the Ostergard file and switched the phone to his left ear, because the right one was still a tad sore about the earlobe.

"Whether an attorney leaves a case isn't up to the client, Jane. You send him the explanatory letter, and you file the motion."

"I know that," she spat, for of course, he should not have presumed to lecture her on legal procedure. "I told him I had a potential conflict of interest I hadn't known about when I took the case, and I'm ethically required to get out of the case."

Not a potential conflict of interest, a real conflict. Dunstan hardly blamed her for putting it more delicately to her client. He would put it the same way to Doreen.

"And?"

"He said he'd waive the conflict. Seems accountants deal with conflict of interest occasionally too."

"Bloody hell. I haven't been able to reach Doreen. Let me think."

"How's your back?"

His back? He'd found the sure cure for his back, though the interlude with Jane played hell with his conscience.

"My back is fine, thank you. Chili for breakfast is my new favorite medicinal."

A silence fell, awkward, wishful. They spoke at the same time.

"I've been meaning to make something clear—" From Jane.

"Would you ever consider—?" From Dunstan.

He did not want to endure whatever she'd been meaning to make clear, because women who wanted more from a man they'd spent the night with—the night loving him to exhaustion—didn't sneak off in the morning, then wait three days to call the fellow.

"If you have to be specific with Calvin," Dunstan said, "then be specific. We were both in that bed, Jane, and we're both adults. I'll be getting out of the case too, as soon as I can get Doreen to return my calls."

"Divorce clients are like that," she said. "They bombard you with calls over nothing, then go to ground when you need an urgent signature."

She'd probably complained about that to the absent Louise, while Dunstan griped to his cat about the same thing.

"This isn't urgent," Dunstan said. "Nobody has filed anything."

Back to the legalities, when he wanted to ask her if she was wearing shoes, and if so, were they the spiky kind or the little black slippers.

"When are you supposed to meet with Calvin again?" he asked, though why wouldn't a guy with his hand in the till, or hiding marital assets, be eager to delay the divorce proceedings any way he could?

"He said he'd get back to me, but that I'm staying in the case."

"Did he tell you why?" Though Dunstan knew why: Jane was damned good.

If she were subjected to disciplinary action because of something Dunstan could have prevented, he would not forgive himself.

"He said I'm not in it for the money."

"Smart man. You're not, but why did he say that?" Dunstan considered switching the phone again—his left earlobe had some residual soreness too—but he liked the reminder of what Jane DeLuca could do when wearing no shoes.

"I'm forever badgering him to get into counseling. For himself, for Doreen, for the kids. The family's entire upkeep lands on Calvin's shoulders, and I don't want my guy to fall apart."

And her client sensed that, sensed her concern.

"I've told Doreen the same thing. She doesn't think Calvin will spend the money."

The silence was more thoughtful, more lawyerly, and sadder.

"That loneliness stuff again," Jane said. "Making fools of us."

"Jane, promise me you won't do anything rash or heroic. It wasn't loneliness—" His second line beeped. "Hold on. This might be Doreen."

"I'll wait."

Dunstan hit the rollover line button, half-hoping it was Doreen.

"We still on for lunch?" MacKenzie Knightley, the guy everybody took to lunch when they had a tough criminal case to deal with.

"Hello, Mac. I'd forgotten we'd scheduled lunch today." Forgotten pretty much everything having to do with running a law office.

"Now or never," Mac said. "I have an attempted murder coming up for trial, and my dance card is getting full. We can reschedule, but don't expect me to desecrate poker night with shop talk."

The light on Dunstan's first line winked out.

Bloody hell.

"Of course not. Poker night is so I can listen to three grown men fret over what to get one small girl for Christmas." For Trenton Knightley's daughter had no more devoted uncles than Mac and James.

"So listen to me fret over lunch too," Mac said. "I'm in the mood for something besides a chicken salad or a tuna melt."

"Mexican," Dunstan said, because the only person he'd eat Eritrean with—the person he'd gladly surrender his license to practice law for—had just hung up on him.

CHAPTER FIVE

"*Louise?*" Jane was so surprised to see her former partner she'd inadvertently pushed the wrong button and cut Dunstan off instead of putting him on hold. "Damn, your timing stinks. Take a load off and gimme a minute to finish this call."

She started to redial, then realized Louise would overhear every word, and Louise was still a member of the bar. As in, Louise could be questioned in connection with any grievance brought against another member of the bar.

Thinking like a lawyer sometimes sucked rotten eggs.

"Tough case?" Louise asked as Jane put the receiver back on its cradle.

"Yes—no. Yes and no. How have you been?"

"Art school is wonderful."

The school was up in York, Pennsylvania, better than an hour's drive on a chilly, sloppy day, and Louise was not giving off the wonderful vibe.

"And?"

"And I'm thinking of quitting the job."

Jane came around the desk to take the second guest chair. "Lou, you saved for years to make this jump. You put up with Judge Mansfield, did DUIs until your eyes crossed, and you're thinking of throwing in the towel? Does this have to do with a man?"

Louise examined her nails, which were naked—not lacquered, polished, or even manicured. Clay was her favorite medium, and hard on the hands.

"Maybe with the absence of a man. Robert informed me last week he's considering a design job in New York."

New York was the brass ring in the design field, the Holy Grail, the Supreme Court of the United States—according to the designers working in New York.

"Bastard."

"Oh, maybe, but I shouldn't have changed careers to chase a guy."

"I didn't think you were."

Louise was a beautiful woman. Tall, with dark auburn hair, chocolate-brown eyes, and a killer figure, she should have been an artist's model, if nothing else.

And she was sad, which on her had the gall to look even prettier.

"I didn't think I was chasing a guy, either," she said. "But now Robert's off for the bright lights, and I'm left in good old P-A, trying not to wince every time somebody says 'you-inz' and wondering what was so awful about the practice of law."

Robert was an okay guy, but he didn't look at Louise the way Louise looked at fresh clay and an afternoon free to spend with her wheel.

"You're thinking of transferring to a school in New York?"

Louise rose and went to the dish garden, testing the dampness of the moss with her finger, then using Eeyore to give the moss a drink.

"That hadn't even occurred to me. Do you have court this afternoon?"

"No." Thank God. Because at the courthouse, she might run into Dunstan, and that would be lovely and awful and difficult and wonderful. Until she was out of the Almquist case, a dram of avoidance would be worth a cask of disbarment.

"If you don't have court, then let's go to lunch," Louise said, shrugging back into her coat.

"Lou, I was in the middle of a phone call. An important phone call."

"Whoever it was didn't call you back, did they?" She tossed Jane her coat and shouldered Jane's carpetbag. "Call them after lunch, because I need somebody to talk sense into me, and you're all I've got."

"We'll discuss a hypothetical or two, because I need some sense talked into me too."

"No, you don't. You aren't the risk-taking kind, and that's why you didn't waste thousands of dollars relocating for an adjunct position so you could teach drawing to a bunch of fashionably emaciated waifs ten years your junior."

"We used to be waifs, Lou. Where are we going?" Jane had to hustle, because Louise on a mission was a long-legged, fast-moving train.

"Someplace spicy. Cold weather works up my appetite, and I haven't found any decent restaurants yet near school. Why didn't I think of offering to go to New York with Robert?"

"I dunno. If a certain Scotsman told me he was heading home, I would at least hint about a willingness to visit him there."

Louise slowed to Mach One. "A *Scotsman*?"

Jane grabbed her by the elbow when she would have stepped off the curb. "Mexican's the closest. Tell me about these guys ten years younger than you."

The distraction worked, at least temporarily, but Jane hadn't been entirely honest with her friend.

If Dunstan went back to Scotland to stay, Jane would offer to go with him, and hang the immigration laws.

Hang all the damned laws.

* * *

"So how're things?" Mac asked. "Has Judge Blaisdale quoted any Shakespeare at you lately?"

When Blaisdale got out the Shakespeare, somebody's client was going down hard in the yard, as the denizens of the Detention Center put it.

"Not for a couple weeks," Dunstan replied. "You're having a taco salad? How is that different from a chicken salad?" And which case was it that had prompted Dunstan to schedule lunch with MacKenzie Knightley?

"I'm having a taco salad with rice and beans. Carbohydrates fuel the brain," Mac said, catching the waitress's eye.

Carby bliss fueled the brain.

"May we have some lemon for our water?" Mac asked. Nothing about MacKenzie Knightley was flirtatious—not one damned thing—but the waitress beamed at him as if his every wish was her darkest fantasy come true.

"How do you do that?" Dunstan asked, tucking his tie away. "How do you appeal to the ladies without so much as batting your eyes?"

Mac took a sip of Dos Equis—no heather ale here. "Maybe the ladies can sense I'm no threat. I'm not buying, they don't have to sell, and we can all relax."

Dunstan could not relax. Why had Jane hung up on him?

"Attempted murder keeps you warm at night?"

"The woodstove keeps me warm at night, Cromarty, and most other times. You have lady trouble."

Dunstan left off staring at the beer menu—whose idea had it been to do Mexican?—while Mac watched him patiently.

"How ever can you tell such a thing, MacKenzie?"

Mac waited until the smiling waitress dropped off a dish of lemon wedges arranged in an artful pinwheel.

"I have two little brothers, one of whom has been through such a nasty divorce, he's practically a monk. The other is the equivalent of a temple whore, stepping out with any dumped, divorced, or desperate woman. I know when the ladies are giving a guy fits, Cromarty. Sooner or later, everybody gets a turn in that barrel."

Which left the question of when Mac had taken his turn, or was he still taking it?

"So let's consider a hypothetical," Dunstan said. "Family law case, two competent attorneys, parties still talking but not exactly cordial. The money isn't adding up, somebody has income they're not disclosing, probably opposing counsel's client, and opposing counsel may or may not know what's afoot. The lawyers have a wee, private lapse and get a bit too affectionate on one occasion—"

"You get out of the case," Mac said. "You both get your sorry, besotted, unethical asses out of the case, and you never, ever oppose each other—unless you're James Knightley."

"*What?*"

Mac squeezed three lemon wedges over his water glass. Something about the dispatch with which he pulverized his citrus reminded Dunstan that the guy also shoed horses.

"Trent and I have our suspicions about our baby brother, and it's all but bar association fact the state's attorney was tying 'em on with Danica Showalter before she went to rehab."

Danica was—had been—a criminal defense attorney. Nobody seemed to know what had become of her after her second trip through rehab.

"Am I supposed to derive comfort from the notion that our very own bar association is less than angelic?"

"Yes," Mac said, passing the remaining lemons over to Dunstan. "You're also supposed to get out of the case."

The pretty pinwheel wasn't half so appealing with three mangled wedges among its number.

"The clients in this purely hypothetical example aren't cooperating. One has said he'll waive any conflict, though the exact nature of the problem hasn't yet been explained to him. I suspect the second will follow suit."

Mac again waited until the food had been set on the table, such was his inherent discretion.

"Eat your food, Cromarty. Though why anybody would go to a Mexican restaurant and tell them to hold the rice and beans, I do not know. Who has your knickers in an uproar?"

Not his knickers, his earlobes, his law practice, everything between his earlobes, and his—

The cheery little bell over the door jingled, and who should walk in, but Jane DeLuca and her former law partner. Dunstan wanted to wave, wanted to tackle the woman where she stood—in furry brown boots with low heels—but instead, he took a bite of whatever he'd ordered.

"We were discussing a hypothetical, Mac." For Jane either hadn't seen him, or was ignoring him altogether.

"Cromarty, stop looking pathetic. You're a grown man, and if Jane DeLuca has given you the time of day, so to speak, you're the first to breach that citadel in living memory."

"I would also like to be the last." If nothing else had come clear during the past three days of mooning at his phone like a lovesick juvenile, that had.

"Your clients are in the middle of a divorce when they themselves are likely tempted by all sorts of stupid impulses. Yes, the bar association will take a dim view of what has happened, but you'll probably get away with a suspension—a pair of suspensions."

Across the busy restaurant, Jane slid into a booth opposite Louise. Coats were shuffled aside, the Mary Poppins rucksack stayed by Jane's side, and beneath the table, her boots remained on her feet.

"Jane DeLuca will not be suspended. I'll turn in my license before I'll allow that to happen."

"Then the condemned should enjoy a last meal. What did you order anyway?"

"Food." Dunstan put a twenty on the table. "I hope you and Louise get along, because I'm kidnapping a member of the bar for nefarious purposes."

"Those are the best kind," Mac said, slipping the twenty into his wallet. "Kidnapping is a felony, please recall."

Dunstan left Mac sipping his beer and muttering a line from *MacBeth*: *Confusion now hath made his masterpiece.*

* * *

"Ladies, hello."

Jane left off fishing for tissues in The Vast Lonely, because that voice was the last one she'd expected to hear.

Her Every Stupid Wish loomed over the table, looking serious, tired, and dear. "Dunstan. A pleasure to see you. You and Louise know each other?"

"Of course we do, though MacKenzie Knightley is in want of a lunch companion, and I was hoping Louise would oblige."

"What are friends for?" Louise said, abandoning the field without giving Jane a chance to tromp on her foot under the table. "Mac is always good company."

She was across the restaurant in half a heartbeat.

"And what am I?" Jane muttered, "chopped livva?"

"You are coming with me," Dunstan said. "You don't leave a man with sore earlobes and then not call him for three days."

Across the restaurant, Louise waved while MacKenzie Knightley saluted with his beer and winked.

"Please, Jane. Will you walk with me?"

"We are still counsel of record," Jane hissed, scooting out of the booth. "You can't tell me about your earlobes, and I can't tell you about my—"

He held her coat for her, just as if they were a couple of longstanding. "Your what?"

With her back to him, she could interrupt her flight of lawyer nerves to ask, "Why didn't you call me?"

His hands stroked over her shoulders, fleetingly. "One doesn't want to presume."

She turned and flipped her hair out of her collar. "Bull-poo-poo, Cromarty."

"Very well," he said, preceding her to the door and holding it for her. "I wanted to get out of the case before I contacted you again. That plan isn't working."

"We are in such doo-doo," Jane said, while Dunstan scooted around her to take the position closer to the street.

"No, we are not," Dunstan retorted, with the air of a man who had spent all night rehearsing his closing argument.

And then somebody's phone chimed to the tune of *Scotland the Brave*.

"Fook."

"At least it's not Dixie," Jane said, while Dunstan held his phone to his ear.

He went still, dark brows drawing down. "Yes, Doreen. I'll contact Ms. DeLuca. Two o'clock?"

He shot Jane a questioning glance, and she nodded, for this afternoon she had neither clients nor court appearances nor common sense.

"My office, then, and yes, I'll make sure Ms. DeLuca's there too."

He slipped his phone into a pocket, while Jane tried to memorize what was good about the moment, for it might be among their last as practicing attorneys. Dunstan's expression was impassive, blaming nobody, and that was good.

Jane was healthy, had some cash stashed, and no ficus plant depending on her.

That was good too.

"Wallace can survive a long time on half rations," she said. "And I want to take your hand right here on the street. Those are good things, Dunstan. I don't eat much when I'm nervous, and that's probably a good thing too. I have tissues in my purse, and that's a very good thing."

Dunstan was a resourceful guy. He didn't take her hand, there on the street for all to see, but he winged his elbow, like an old-fashioned gentleman might, when the way was slippery, and a lady could fall on her backside at any moment.

* * *

"Doreen and Calvin would like to meet with us," Dunstan said, though that wasn't quite accurate. Doreen had *demanded* another four-way meeting and had said Calvin would confirm that request with his attorney if necessary.

Calvin, whose position earlier had been to waive any conflicts of interest, was now demanding a four-way meeting.

"Here's another good thing," Jane said. "When I'm in a situation where my law practice can be taken from me, I realize I like being a lawyer. Yes, we have hard days, but what goes on in the courthouse is a big improvement over the ducking stool and the lynch mob. I like being part of solving people's legal problems."

Such comforting images, the ducking stool and the lynch mob.

"This is what we tell our clients, then," Dunstan said. "We tell them I made untoward advances to you, and that's why we're getting out of the case. You can report me to the bar association, and they'll slap my wrist,"—probably with the disciplinary equivalent of a sledgehammer—"and I'll be able to sleep at night."

Maybe even with Jane?

She stopped right in the middle of the sidewalk. "That would be lying, Dunstan. I'm the one who propositioned you."

American English was not a language for the faint of heart.

"You extended an invitation, which I was more than free to decline, Jane. Both of us need not suffer the consequences."

She got the same look in her eye she'd had when Dunstan had told her to run along.

"Dunstan, do you *want* to be sent back to Scotland with your tail between your legs? Do you *want* to spend the next twenty years teaching the same constitutional law cases at the Podunk Highland School of Law and Hangover Remedies?"

He took her arm and resumed their stroll toward the legal gallows.

"Here we come to one of your good things, though why you'd focus on such a litany at this juncture, I do not know. Now, when I'm faced with losing my livelihood, and returning to Scotland is the only reasonable choice, I find instead I want to buy the house I'm living in, get Wallace some company for the long days he's stuck at home, and otherwise anchor myself here more thoroughly."

Jane was part of that, but not all of it. Taking a cat to Europe was no easy feat.

"But Scotland is home," Jane said, ever the advocate—for anybody but herself. "Scotland is where you have nieces and nephews and the wee whatevers, and everybody can understand you when you cuss."

"You can understand me when I don't cuss. You can understand me when I don't say anything at all."

He should not have said that. Jane fell silent, no argument, no motions, no cross-examination as they ambled along.

"We're not lying to our clients, Dunstan. That's not the kind of lawyers we are."

Now was his turn to argue, to point out that if they put the bald truth on the table, they wouldn't be any kind of lawyers at all. They waited on a corner for the light to change, though no traffic moved in either direction.

"You're sure, Jane?"

A leaf drifted by, one of the last golden remnants of the venerable oak.

"I would like to see Scotland someday," she said. "I'd like that a lot. I can't imagine an entire country where everybody sounds like you."

Well, then. He walked along beside his Jane, a lightness suffusing him, despite the afternoon's agenda.

Get fired.

Refund an entire retainer despite hours spent on the case.

Begin long, messy, ultimately costly disciplinary proceedings.

Shut down a law practice after years of trying to build it up.

And finish falling in love.

Not a bad day's work.

He stopped outside the building housing Jane's office, which was around the block from his. "I'll see you at two. Mind you, don't leave me to face the dragons alone."

As if she would.

Jane stretched up to kiss his cheek. "Until two."

* * *

What sort of man offers to ruin his career for a single night of—

Not sex.

Lovemaking? And cuddling, and talking. And more lovemaking, and sore earlobes, and sore…

Jane took the place across from Dunstan at his lovely conference table and pulled the Almquist file out of her bag, the Complaint for Limited Divorce right on top. Dunstan had on his glasses, his yellow legal pad at the ready, business as usual—except this was every lawyer's worst nightmare.

And he was ready to face it with her.

"This shouldn't take long," Calvin said.

Across the table, Dorie watched him, and not with the guarded, bitchy expression of a woman preparing to do battle. She wore jeans and a UMBC sweatshirt, while Cal was in jeans, a blue button-down, and a tan corduroy jacket.

Counseling, then. They'd finally started counseling. Dunstan must have sensed this too, because under the stable, a large foot gently nudged at Jane's boot.

"We have as much time as you need," Dunstan said. "And we're not on the clock."

Of course they weren't. Jane nudged him back: *Good call.*

"Tell them, Cal," Dorie said. "It's not complicated."

No, it was not, though where was Calvin's triple-steel reinforced Underwriters Laboratory-approved briefcase?

"My attorney said something that got me thinking," Calvin said. "Jane said that I hadn't kept a close enough eye on the household account. I'm the accountant in the family, and I leave all that for Dorie to manage."

"I don't mind," Dorie said. "You put in enough hours with the numbers."

They exchanged a look, a married-couple-shorthand look Jane couldn't quite fathom. Divorces weren't always nasty, though they were usually sad, and that look had held regret, at least.

"In any case," Calvin went on, "I couldn't get that observation out of my mind, and I began to look, really look, at what it takes to keep our house going. Having a new water heater installed on an emergency basis was hundreds of dollars. If we'd picked one up ourselves, and I'd taken a Saturday morning to install it—the boys would have helped, would have learned a few things."

A regret phase then, but where were the Almquists headed with this?

"Cal asked to see the checkbook," Dorie said, spreading her hands out flat on the conference table. Today her nails were plain, and she wore no rings—suggesting they'd found a *good* counselor. "At first I thought Cal was snooping, looking for how I'd wasted his hard-earned money."

"Our hard-earned money," Cal interjected.

"But then I figured, he's still my husband, and we won't get through this divorce by stealing from each other. I showed him the real checkbook."

Dunstan shot Jane a perplexed look, but kept his thoughts and his toes to himself.

"Dorie keeps excellent records," Cal said. "I'm an accountant, and I couldn't see what any fool would have seen."

"I didn't want you to see, Vinnie."

"And I can't see," Jane said. "What did you find in those records, Calvin?"

"I found my wife."

Across the table, husband and wife visually held hands. Dunstan saw it too, because he pushed his yellow legal pad aside, put his pen down, and took off his glasses.

"My lawyer, who has never set foot in my house, picked up on what I'd been blind to," Calvin said. "One income isn't enough to sustain the lifestyle we enjoy. Dorie has been tutoring college kids in English, and what I assumed were trips to the gym, lunches with the ladies, and tennis games were Dorie's way of bringing in extra money without making me feel inadequate."

"It's not that much," Dorie said. "And I like helping young people learn. I have a master's in English, and I wasn't doing anything with it. And I would have told Cal soon, because we file our taxes jointly. A 1099 is a tough thing to hide from a CPA. Besides, Dunstan saw the same thing Jane did and was about to go all lawyer on the household financial records. I'd rather Cal learned the truth from me."

"I lost sight of my marriage, but Dorie is right: I would have noticed a statement of income earned, but I'd become blind to my own wife. What does that say about me and my own accountability?"

"It says you're human," Dunstan suggested. "Does this mean you'll go to counseling?"

Dorie tucked her hair back behind her ear, a curiously girlish gesture. "It means we went to bed—well, the utility closet first. And the shower, and then—"

"Sweetie." Calvin's tone was indulgent—or smug? "I don't think a pair of divorce lawyers needs to know those details."

"No," Jane said. "We don't." *The utility closet?* "So where do you want to go from here with the lawsuit?"

"Nowhere," Dorie replied. "Cal will telecommute two days a week outside of tax season, I'll try to limit my tutoring to the other three days, and we'll get back to being married."

"You might still consider counseling," Dunstan said.

"Maybe." The look in Cal's eyes promised his wife more trips to the utility closet too.

"I'll be getting my checkbook, then," Dunstan said, rising. "And I'll forward to Doreen the contents of the file after I've had a chance to copy them."

When the door had closed, Doreen appropriated Dunstan's legal pad and pen and began to doodle.

"Is there any point telling that man to keep his checkbook?" she asked.

"None, and I have mine with me too," Jane said, though it took a moment of fishing to find it. "I'm happy for you folks. This doesn't happen often, but I'm always glad when it does."

Calvin sidled around the table to take the seat Dunstan had vacated. "I liked that about you, that you pushed me toward reconciliation and counseling."

"I don't always," Jane said, scrawling out a check. "Each case is different. Then too, sometimes the devil you know is the very best devil for you."

She pushed the check across to Calvin, who had to inspect the amount.

"This is for the full retainer," he said. "That's not what we agreed to. I'm happy to pay—"

Doreen put her hand over his mouth. "Say thank you, Calvin."

He kissed her fingers, and Jane nearly had to open a window. "Thank you, Jane, but why?"

Tell the client the truth that matters most. "Because this case has done my heart good."

Doreen left off flirting with her husband long enough to peer at Jane. "Dunstan's not a bad-looking guy, you know, though he's a little on the imposing side. He seems kinda lonely to me, all work and no play. You two might get along. You should think about it."

Jane was preserved from stammering a reply when the not-bad-looking guy himself came back into the room, check in hand.

"Best of luck, folks," he said, handing Dorie her refund.

"Now, see what I mean?" Dorie said. "This is for the full amount too, and you two didn't even have to consult each other about it. You might get along with each other better than you think. Honey, put this in the Christmas fund, would you?"

"I think we should start a second-honeymoon fund," Calvin said, getting to his feet and tucking the check away. "Or maybe an annual honeymoon fund."

"Out," Dunstan said, pointing toward the door. "And never come back, because we willna represent you for any amount of money. Consider Scotland for one of those holidays, though. It's beautiful any time of year."

Doreen took Calvin by the hand, patted Dunstan's cheek, and winked at Jane.

And then they were gone.

Saved by the utility closet.

* * *

"Is Scotland lovely any time of year?" Jane asked, tossing her checkbook into that great bag of hers.

What was she really asking?

"Depends on what part of Scotland. One area in the northwest gets close to sixteen feet of rainfall a year. A lot of our sadder, drunker ballads are from that region."

"I'm neither sad nor drunk," Jane said, running her fingers over the surface of the conference table. "I'm really, really relieved."

Dunstan took the place beside her, purely for the pleasure of proximity to her, not because his own knees were feeling weak. "We had a near miss."

"I don't like that I put the cart before the horse," Jane said. "I should have kept my pants on, withdrawn from the case, then jumped your bones."

He prayed there was a but coming. "I'm not proud of myself in that regard, either."

"Is there a but coming?"

Dunstan could tell from how Jane scooted a bit that beneath the table, she was shuffling off her boots.

"Yes. Yes, there is a but, or a however. We're good at what we do, Jane."

"Very good, which excuses nothing."

The temptation to take her hand was nearly befuddling him, but he wanted to put his reasoning before her.

"We both know the rules, and for my part, when you gave me the opportunity, I put a higher value on sharing intimacies with you than I did on my continued ability to practice law."

The grain of the chestnut surface apparently fascinated Jane, because she studied it as if it were an original manuscript of the first Supreme Court opinion handed down.

"Jane?"

"What you're saying is, if you had it to do over again, even knowing we might be disbarred, even knowing it wasn't smart or professional, you would have done the same thing—and so would I. What does that say about us, Dunstan? As attorneys, sworn to uphold the law, as officers of the court?"

The answer to her question had kept him up for two nights, and it did matter—some.

"It says the law is important to us, but we're more important to each other. In this one instance, I can live with that revelation. I can even rejoice in it. I've never misstepped like this before, Jane, and I certainly don't intend to again."

He trapped her hand in his, lest she stroke the finish right off the conference table.

She turned her hand palm up and laced her fingers with his. "I'm not as ethical as you are."

The hell she wasn't. "I cannot believe you've ever before taken opposing counsel—"

Her free hand covered his mouth.

"I want to misstep *with you* a lot, Dunstan. This is a problem. We're in a small jurisdiction, and the family law bar is smaller yet. We should have opposed each other at least twice a year, and why that hasn't happened, I do not know."

"You were willing to toss aside your license to practice law to have at my earlobes, and now you're not willing to pass on the occasional case because I might oppose you? You'll let yourself have a taste of something wonderful, then go back to chicken salad on wilted lettuce?"

"I had another option in mind."

Options were good. The more options, the greater the likelihood of settlements. "I'm listening." And holding her hand too tightly.

"I was hoping Louise would change her mind about art school, but she's off to New York next semester, or somewhere. My office is set up for two attorneys, and I hate to do the billing."

He brought her hand to his lips and kissed her knuckles. "You are a fraud, Jane DeLuca. A lovely, brilliant little fraud. Beneath that calculating legal mind beats the heart of a true romantic."

"I really do hate the billing."

A true, honest romantic. He tucked her hair back, the better to see the woman he loved. "Are you sure about this? Because clearly, my house has room for a home office."

She regarded their joined hands solemnly. "Do you have a utility closet?"

"Aye. How do you feel about scheduled sex?"

She glanced at the clock. "I'm okay with it, occasionally. Maybe around 2:53 p.m.?"

"I had 2:55 p.m. in mind because we have one more item to cover in our first partners' meeting. Will you come to Scotland with me over the holidays? Meet the family, dandle a few bairnies, flirt with Uncle Donald?"

"Yes." She inched her chair closer. "This all feels very sudden, and very right."

He gave up her hand for the pleasure of putting his arms around her. "That it does, but you should be warned, I'm no' asking you to travel home with me simply to show off Scotland."

"I'd love to see Scotland."

"I'm scheduling a proposal, too, Jane DeLuca. I want to propose to you on my home turf, when I can tell my family if you've accepted and have my choice of fine whiskeys to console me if you turn me down."

She kissed his cheek. "Does the conference room door lock?"

"Aye. Why?"

"Because it's 2:55 p.m., and I've had ideas about this conference table since I first laid eyes on it."

Dunstan locked the door, and they held the longest partners' meeting in the history of the Damson County bar association.

–THE END–

Dunroamin Holiday

GRACE BURROWES

DEDICATION

Dedicated to my late brother-in-law, Dr. Thomas Edwards Polk, II, PhD. Tom gave me the first sincere compliment I can recall receiving, and since that day (I was about eleven), I've stood a little taller and been a little more confident.

CHAPTER ONE

"Scottish men are hot, fun, and emotionally unavailable," the travel agent chirped. "Exactly what a girl needs for the perfect vacation."

Louise Cameron hadn't been a girl for years, while the woman madly typing on the other side of the desk—Hi, I'm Cindy!—looked like she'd yet to graduate high school.

"I need peace and quiet," Louise said, "which is why I'll spend my time in a cottage in the Scottish countryside, more or less by myself."

The agent, a perky exponent of the more-highlights-are-better school of cosmetology, swiveled away from her keyboard as a printer purred out an itinerary.

"The Scottish countryside is full of men, braw, bonnie laddies who can hold their whisky, so to speak. Hit the nearest pub and wear dancing shoes. You know the tickets are nonrefundable?"

The question gave Louise a pang. "The charges have already hit my credit card." Jane had insisted as only Jane could, and in a weak moment of rebound impulsivity, Louise had capitulated.

Nonrefundable tickets were cheaper, and a woman who'd abandoned the lucrative practice of law needed to watch her piggy bank—or return to the practice of law.

"Then you're all set!" Hi-I'm-Cindy! snatched the itinerary from the printer, tucked it into an envelope, and slid the packet across the desk. "Let me know if you have a good time, though I'm sure you will. Scotland is one of the fastest-growing travel destinations on the planet and for good reason. We've had nothing but rave reviews for Dunroamin Cottage, and the scenery is unbelievable, if you know what I mean."

Before Louise could be subjected to a lascivious wink, she stuffed the itinerary and tickets into her purse and rose.

"Thanks, Cindy. I'll tell the braw, kilted laddies you said hello. I'm off to lunch." With the author of Louise's latest misfortune.

Jane had already chosen a table when Louise arrived at their favorite Eritrean restaurant—also the only Eritrean restaurant in Damson Valley.

"Greetings, earthling!" Jane said, bouncing to her feet and kissing Louise's cheek. "If you bailed on your Scottish vacation, I will sue the travel agent."

Jane looked better than ever, her red hair longer than Louise recalled seeing it, her petite figure every bit as perfect. Jane's recent marriage to, and law practice merger with, Dunstan Cromarty was probably responsible for the damned twinkle in her eyes.

"I didn't bail," Louise said. She hadn't bailed *yet*. "What are you working on?"

Lawyer-fashion, Jane had papers spread out on the table. As Louise slid into the booth, Jane gathered up the documents and tucked them into a plain manila folder.

"Big bad divorce proceeding," Jane muttered.

"The best kind." From a billable hours perspective. "Anybody I know?"

Louise flipped open a menu rather than glance at the name on the folder, though as often as she and Jane had eaten here, Louise could have recited the entrees from the depths of a Chunky Monkey coma.

Jane stashed the paperwork in a shoulder bag that had been known to double as a gym bag, emergency first aid bag, overnight bag, and gourmet goodie bag.

"Nothing's been filed yet," Jane said.

Meaning Louise, because she didn't actively practice with Jane any more, wasn't privy to the details.

"I'm still legally a partner in the firm," Louise said. "Besides, I'm off to Scotland for the next several weeks, and won't have anybody to gossip with."

People underestimated Jane because she was diminutive and pretty. As an attorney, she was also hell in stilettos when she chose to be. That she'd teamed up in every way with Dunstan Cromarty made sense: The big Scot was up to Jane's weight, so to speak.

"Julie Leonard is ditching the handsome buffoon she married in a fit of madness right out of law school," Jane said, squeezing lemon into her water.

"Julie has always been a pleasure to work with." To the extent that a prosecutor could *be* a pleasure to work with when she was trying to put your client behind bars. "Maybe Madam State's Attorney needs a Scottish vacation, too."

Or a Scottish honeymoon. Jane had truly never looked better, for which Louise ought to hate the entire country. Louise pretended to study the menu instead, though her appetite hadn't been spotted since about Christmas.

"Have you heard from Robert?" Jane asked.

Let the cross-examination begin. "Yes, I have. He's engaged."

"I'm sorry." Jane's compassion was immediate and sincere, also irritating as hell.

"It's my past all over again," Louise said, putting the menu aside. "I fall for an art professor and he screws me over. The last one stole my glazing process, and this one leaves me with three months on the lease, and for a sophomore whose understanding of art depends on having a mouse in her hand—of one species or another."

"A wee, sleekit, cow'rin, tim'rous beastie, that mouse," Jane smirked. "You're better off without him."

Brilliant legal deduction. "Let's order, shall we?"

They had their usual—sambusas, soup, and plenty of warm, vinegary injera bread. Louise ate to avoid a scolding, not because the food appealed.

"Lou, are you okay?"

Well, hell. "I will be. The soup is good, don't you think?"

"Louise Mavis Cameron, I am your friend, so stop being polite. If you don't want to teach drawing anymore, then don't. If you don't want to practice law ever again, that's okay, too. A big, wide world will surely offer something you enjoy doing that pays the bills. While you try to figure out what that is, go to Scotland. Dunstan says Wallace will enjoy having some feline company while you're gone."

Louise dipped her spoon in the soup of the day and said nothing. How pathetic was it, that her sole excuse for canceling a very expensive trip abroad came down to the abiding fear that she'd miss her cat?

* * *

"You should feel sorry for the lass," Jeannie said, turning up the burner under the tea kettle. "She's a lawyer, a spinster, a Yank, and her hobby is throwing pots. Such a blighted soul is surely in need of holidays. She's probably scrimped for years to afford a few weeks in Scotland."

Liam Cromarty felt sorry for *himself*, which unmanly sentiment, Jeannie—a relatively new mother and one of Liam's favorite cousins—would sniff out before the tea kettle had come to a boil.

"Have Uncle Donald show your spinster around then," Liam suggested, plucking an apple from the bowl of fruit on Jeannie's counter. "He's a hopeless flirt, he knows every back road and ruined castle in every shire, and he'll raise her spirits with naughty jokes."

Jeannie took down two mugs, one a bright floral ceramic—Morag's work—the other clear Scandinavian glass. When a baby joined a household, apparently every manifestation of order and organization was imperiled.

"Liam, for shame," Jeannie said, slouching onto a stool at the kitchen counter. "Donald would put the lady in waders and drag her to the nearest trout stream where she'd be pestered crazy by the midgies."

"Donald would also ply the poor dear with good whisky. Sounds like a fine time to me."

The baby on Jeannie's shoulder began to fuss, so Liam plucked him from his mother's grasp.

"Hush, laddie. We'll take you fishing soon enough." The wee fellow peered at Liam from the blue, blue eyes common to Cromarty men of every age. "You must learn to be quiet though, for Donald takes a dim view of a boy who scares away the fishies."

"The little ones always behave for you," Jeannie said, a touch of envy in her tone. "Every bairnie in the family takes to you, no matter how you grouse and brood. You need a holiday too, Liam."

Jeannie was the cousin closest to Liam in age, and more than that, she was his friend. When he'd nearly disappeared into the bottle after Karen's death, Jeannie hadn't given up on him, and for that Liam would always owe her.

He loved her too, and was glad she'd found a man to share her life with.

Truly, he was.

"Can't you ask Morag?" Liam said. "She's the logical choice, being the family potter."

Liam rubbed wee Henry's back, earning a milky-scented baby sigh near his ear. The feel of the child in his arms provoked sentiments ranging from despair to fury to something so tender and vast, he—a man who made his living with words—didn't even try to find a label for it.

"Morag has to build up inventory for this summer," Jeannie said. "She's at her wheel and kiln all the livelong day, and she's not the cheeriest soul."

The kettle whistled, and Jeannie hopped off her stool while Liam continued to rub the boy's back. Morag was a right terror on her bad days. Even when she danced, she brought a ferocity to her grace that Liam understood perhaps better than she'd guess.

The ink was barely dry on Morag's divorce decree. Now was not the time to impose.

"When is this poor refugee from the American legal system to grace Caledonia's shores?"

Liam should not have asked. Jeannie's smile said as much, for the question implied that Liam was rearranging his schedule, making yet another effort to accommodate the vast Cromarty family network. Every auntie, cousin, and in-law assumed a man without wife and children was on call to make up the numbers socially, pitch in on the weekend projects with the menfolk, and otherwise step and fetch on command.

All because they couldn't bear for him to be lonely, of course.

Liam could have told them that activity and family gatherings didn't cure loneliness—something the American spinster probably understood too.

"What does it say about me," he murmured to the child, "that I have something in common with elderly lady lawyers in need of a holiday?"

A wet, unmistakable noise came from the vicinity of the baby's nappy, while Jeannie poured the tea, and Liam made a mental vow to introduce the American spinster to Uncle Donald.

* * *

The flight from Newark to Edinburgh had been made more bearable by an empty seat to Louise's left, and a little old Scottish lady to her right. Hazel Chapman had once upon a time taken tea with the Queen at one of the Holyroodhouse Palace garden parties, which gatherings were limited to a select few hundred souls whom Her Royal Majesty wanted to honor for civic works.

"I volunteer a lot," Hazel had confided, "because I miss the grandchildren so, but a man must go where there's work, aye?"

Yes, and a woman must too, and that meant another semester teaching drawing, at least. Louise chatted with Hazel through passport control and customs, and as they approached the international arrivals area, endured several invitations to stop by Hazel's wool goods shop in some unpronounceable town in the Highlands.

Hazel referred to her boss as "the laird," and said he lived all by himself in a castle on a loch. Truly, Louise had ended up in Scotland.

They parked their suitcases side by side as Hazel rhapsodized about her whisky fudge recipe—an idea Louise could heartily endorse—but Louise couldn't see anybody holding a sign for "L. Cameron" in the milling crowd.

After making initial arrangements with Jeannie MacDonald, one of Dunstan Cromarty's cousins, Louise had exchanged e-mails with another cousin, Liam Cromarty. She pictured her prospective driver as dour, reliable, and safe. The airport crowd included plenty of sturdy, tweedy-looking older fellows who—

"I'll fetch that for you," said a tall, dark-haired guy in jeans, or at least that's what Louise thought he'd said—to Hazel. The actual words were, "Ah'll fetch 'at for ye," with the intonations in all the wrong places.

While Louise's brain translated, Tall, Dark, and Scottish swiped not Hazel's plain black suitcase, but Louise's larger rainbow-print bag.

"Hold on just a minute," Louise snapped, "you've made a mistake, and that's my bag."

"She's right, dearie," Hazel chimed in helpfully. "Mine's the plain black."

Dark brows knit over a substantial nose. "According to your e-mail, your bag is all over colors," he said—to Hazel—and he still didn't turn loose of the suitcase.

"*My* e-mail," Louise informed him, "said *my* suitcase bears a pastel spectrum print, which it does. Are you Mr. Cromarty?"

He was a big sort of Mr. Cromarty—Liam's son, probably. Not his grandson, because this guy had crow's-feet at the corners of startlingly blue eyes, and a few signs of wear around his mouth. Broad shoulders, long legs, dark hair in need of a trim.

Not at all what Louise had pictured.

"Aye, I'm Liam Cromarty." He released the suitcase to extend a large hand in Louise's direction. "Welcome to Scotland, Miss Cameron."

"She's not the formal type," Hazel supplied as Louise's hand was enveloped in a warm grasp. "Americans aren't, you know. You can call her Louise. I'm Hazel, by the way."

"Pleased to make your acquaintance, Hazel. Will you be traveling with Miss Cameron?"

Louise had trouble understanding Liam Cromarty amid the bustle and noise of the airport, but she could pick up the hopeful note behind his words.

"Gracious, laddie, no," Hazel said. "Harold would have apoplexies if I left him home alone for one more night, and there's my Harold now. Louise, you enjoy your stay. The Edinburgers are nice enough once you get to know them."

Hazel toddled off, halloo'ing at one of those short, sturdy older fellows Louise had planned on having for her driver. Mr. Cromarty seemed sad to see Hazel go—as was Louise.

"Glaswegians are notoriously friendly," he said, picking up Louise's suitcase. "They can't help it any more than they can help naming half their boys Jimmy. Did she natter your ear off for the entire flight?"

The suitcase weighed a ton and had a perfectly functional set of wheels. Scottish guys wrestled telephone poles. Maybe they liked to haul suitcases around too.

"Hazel nattered both of my ears off, showed me pictures of the house where she grew up in Glasgow, the town where she sells wool goods in the Highlands now, and at least four hundred pictures of the grandkiddies," Louise said.

Wee Harry, wee Robbie, and the baby, Agnes. Somewhere east of Iceland, Louise had even started comprehending what Hazel had said.

"I'm a little tired, Mr. Cromarty. Would you mind slowing down?"

"Flying west is easier," he said, adjusting his stride and angling for the doors. "Coming this way you need a bit of time to find your bearings. Are you hungry?"

He moved with the easy grace of a man who could see over the crowds. Louise was tall—almost five foot ten in bare feet—but Mr. Cromarty had nearly six inches on her.

"I'm not that hungry," Louise said. She was too tired to be hungry. "A bottle of water would hit the spot."

They emerged from the airport into a sunny morning, though Louise's body had been expecting the middle of the night.

"Good God, the light," she whispered.

Mr. Cromarty set down her suitcase. "I can lend you my sunglasses once we get to the car."

"Toto, I don't think we're in Maryland anymore," Louise said, shading her eyes. The light poured from the sky, bright, sharp, brilliant in a way at once welcome and unfamiliar.

Either Mr. Cromarty was used to oddball Americans, or he was patient by nature. Louise spun a full, slow circle, letting that light readjust her circadian rhythm, her mood, her spirit. This was light to wake up the body, mind, heart, and soul.

"I might have to take up painting," she said, assaying a smile at her unlikely companion. "Light like this reveals much."

The morning sunshine showed Mr. Cromarty to be north of thirty by a few comfortable years and to have a smile both sad and friendly. Louise could not recall meeting a man with eyes that blue. Those eyes made her want to work with color again, and not simply with line.

"If you want to paint, you must paint," he said. "You're on your holiday. You should spend it as you please. My family has enough artists that we'll find you an easel, brushes, and paints."

He resumed walking, but paused at a curb. "Get in the habit of looking the wrong way before crossing the street, Miss Cameron, or you'll step out in front of a taxi."

On the sidewalk before Louise a white arrow pointed off to the right, underscored by the words, "Look right."

"This is all very different."

"And you're very tired, also hungry and thirsty. The car's this way."

Louise waited until Mr. Cromarty had stepped off the curb, then trundled after him. He knew where he was going, which was why she'd paid Jeannie for his services, and he was easy to spot in a crowd because of his height.

More than his height, though, the way he moved caught Louise's interest.

Liam Cromarty conserved his energy by staying relaxed. Dancers learned this lesson early in their careers or courted injury. As Louise followed him to a small black Mercedes on the ground level of a covered garage, an extraordinary thought emerged from her tired, travel-fried mind.

She'd like Liam Cromarty to model for her.

* * *

Perhaps Scotland could learn a thing or two from the United States about spinsters.

Liam had traveled extensively in the United States, though, and all his lectures and gallery openings and interviews didn't support the theory that American spinsters were on the whole astonishingly pretty, and grace itself in early morning sunshine.

Louise Cameron wore her height regally. She regarded the world from slanting chocolate brown eyes that hinted of both disappointment and determination. Her mouth required study, not only because her accent held beguiling traces of the American South, but also because she didn't speak much, and Liam didn't want to miss what little she said.

"I won't mind if you want to nod off," he said as they tooled away from the airport. Traffic, fortunately, was inbound toward Edinburgh at this hour, while Liam's destination was to the north.

"I didn't travel 3,500 miles so I could take a nap, Mr. Cromarty. Will we cross the Forth Road Bridge?"

"In about ten minutes, traffic permitting. You'll find water in the glove box."

Liam allowed her a bit of crankiness. International travel wasn't for everybody, and she had to be exhausted.

She cracked open a bottle of Highland Spring still and took a delicate sip. "What do you do, Mr. Cromarty, when you aren't driving Americans around?"

She was an attorney. Of course, she'd ask questions.

"I teach art history and art appreciation." The answer Liam gave even friends and family, though that wasn't all he did.

Another sip of water. Miss Cameron's hands on a mere plastic bottle managed to look elegant.

"Do you have a favorite period or artist?" she asked.

"Many, but mostly I'm drawn to particular works. I noticed you'd like to visit Rosslyn Chapel, for example. It's well worth an afternoon and this early in spring, it won't be crowded." Liam enjoyed Rosslyn Chapel because it was quiet, the setting was lovely, and the grounds always had at least one friendly cat.

Jeannie had passed along an itinerary that was a curious mixture of the predictable and the puzzling: Culloden Battlefield and the Robert Burns museum, but also "Glasgow."

The entire city? The Willow Tea Rooms? The School of Design? What did an attorney want to see in "Glasgow"?

Or, "The Highlands," which, when taken with the islands, comprised more than half of Scotland.

"What sort of law do you practice, Miss Cameron?"

"General practice. In a small town that means wills, divorces, barking dogs, contracts, guardianships. Lots of variety."

This recitation did not animate her as the simple morning sunshine had, but then, what manner of people went to court over barking dogs?

"Are you hungry?" Liam asked.

"Probably."

"You're not in the United States, Miss Cameron. Women are expected to eat in Scotland, and we like them better for it."

Her lips quirked. Because Liam was dodging around a lorry, he couldn't tell if she'd been about to smile or grimace.

"The traffic is all backward here," she said. "The fast lane is the slow lane, and we're on the wrong side of the road, and I'm on the wrong side of the car. I like it."

She wouldn't like the gas prices, but then, the distances were generally much smaller in Scotland than in the Unites States.

"You can give driving a try when we get out to the country," Liam suggested. "In a lot of places, we have only one-lane roads and that simplifies driving considerably."

Miss Cameron was daintily, relentlessly, swilling down the entire bottle of water. Each time she'd twist off the cap, take a sip, then replace the cap snugly on the bottle. Her hands were long-fingered and ringless.

She wore no jewelry, in fact, which was either a visual sort of quietness, or a precaution against airport security delays.

"I want to see the places with one-lane roads," she said. "I want to see cows and sheep too."

The lady was decidedly odd, even for an American. "You haven't any of those in Maryland?"

"I want to see them *in this light*, Mr. Cromarty, and we don't have those shaggy, red cows with long horns, at least not that I've seen. Those are *cows*, not some prissy bovine selectively bred to produce low-fat milk and six genetically identical calves a year."

From what Liam could recall of his carnivore days, the Highland cow was exceptionally good eating, too.

"The Forth Road Bridge, Miss Cameron, and to the east of us is the rail bridge."

She fell silent as they crossed over the Firth of Forth estuary. To their right was one of the most photographed bridges in the world, a bright red, century-old marvel of engineering and perpetual maintenance. To cross either the rail bridge or the Forth Road Bridge was to leave Edinburgh behind.

Always welcome, that.

"How much farther?" Miss Cameron asked about ten minutes on. The North Sea danced under morning sunshine to their right, while green hills and the occasional farmstead lay off to the left.

"About an hour, all of it pretty. I picked up some scones on the way to the airport. You're welcome to have at them with me."

"Scones," she murmured, apparently going for a Scottish pronunciation. From her, the word came out halfway between "scuns" and "sco-wans," which was nearly spot-on for Perthshire.

"With butter," Liam said. "You'll find a plastic knife in the bag as well. I'll start with cinnamon, and don't spare the butter."

He'd chosen four different varieties—plain, cinnamon, raspberry, and chocolate chip. Miss Cameron slathered butter all over his, then passed it to him wrapped in a serviette.

"But-ter," she repeated under her breath.

Liam took a bite of very good fresh scone. "Are you mocking me, Miss Cameron? I can show you accents that make mine look like English public school."

Defying both his first and second guesses, she chose plain for herself, though she did apply a decent amount of butter.

"Your voice is like the sunlight to me, Mr. Cromarty. Your accent illuminates vowels and consonants I'd stopped hearing. You make words shine."

Louise Cameron liked the sunlight in Scotland, she liked the driving patterns, and she liked Liam's accent. Perhaps these two weeks wouldn't be such a trial after all.

* * *

Whoever said the occasional modest dose of gluten was bad for the body was an idiot. Louise nibbled fresh-baked heaven, the scone balancing on the edge between bread and pastry, between sinful and delicious.

And the butter had to be organic. But-ter. Mr. Cromarty's elocution was a revelation, a more athletic, energetic rendering of the English alphabet than Louise could muster, plus some vowel sounds she was sure hadn't crossed the Atlantic with the pilgrims.

She opened the second and last bottle of water.

"Thirsty, Mr. Cromarty?"

"A wee nip will do," he said, accepting the bottle from her. The second half of his scone was balanced on his thigh, and he handled the steering wheel and the water bottle easily. No speeding for Mr. Cromarty.

He passed the bottle back, and Louise took a drink before twisting the cap back on. Even the water here tasted—

"Holy Ned," Louise muttered, staring at the bottle. "I can't believe I did that."

Mr. Cromarty maneuvered the car off the four-lane highway and onto a side road.

"Did what? Shared the bottle with me? I'm in good health. We'll be breathing the same air for the next few weeks, touching the same doorknobs. I think you're safe enough, Miss Cameron."

He was laughing at her. Louise was too tired to smack him, and besides, she hadn't figured out how to drive here yet. Liam Cromarty was necessary to her plans, and she liked listening to him.

"Sharing a bottle is biologically comparable to kissing," Louise said. "I don't kiss guys I've just met, no matter how much I enjoy their vowels."

That was the last thing she recalled saying, until a large hand gently shook her shoulder.

"Wake up, Miss Cameron. Welcome to your temporary home."

Louise was in the middle of preparing a Motion to Reconsider while Robert pranced around the courtroom wearing nothing but a Greek drinking vessel on his head.

"I'm not finished," she muttered.

"The rain will start any minute."

Courtrooms suffered excesses of hot air, but no rain. "Go away."

The next thing Louis knew, she was scooped out of the car and hefted against a broad male chest. Her first instinct was to cuddle up to soft wool and woodsy aromas, but she instead heaved open her eyes.

"You, sir, are carrying me." Carrying her up to a little house snuggled among big trees.

"American ladies are a sharp bunch," Mr. Cromarty said, "but they can't hold their scones worth a damn." He deposited Louise on a padded porch swing, produced keys from his jacket pocket, and opened the door just as thunder rumbled off in the distance.

"Welcome to Dunroamin Cottage, Miss Cameron. The temperature's dropping, and we can't have you falling asleep in the wet."

"Give me a minute, please." Or an hour or an entire season.

The sun had fled behind steely clouds, leaving the cottage surrounded by gloom and forest primeval. The leaves had a self-illuminated quality visible only as new foliage passed through the chartreuse phase of unfurling.

The surrounding trees were a mix of conifers and hardwoods, and the yard was mostly rocks and bracken.

Mr. Cromarty picked up Louise's suitcase and disappeared into the cottage. The dwelling was cozy, a two-story stone structure that begged for pots of flowers by day and mysterious dancing lights at twilight.

Thunder sounded again, and a chipper, woodsy breeze gusted through the clearing.

"Shall I start you a fire?" Mr. Cromarty asked, closing the door behind him and rejoining Louise on the porch. "The rain wasn't supposed to start until this afternoon, but Scottish weather has a mind of its own."

"I don't want to go inside," Louise said. "I've always loved storms, and one of the things I didn't like about being a lawyer is that I always worked inside."

Though Louise had only now realized that. Long, long days in the courtroom, sitting, sitting, sitting, and trying to stay mentally sharp in an environment budgeted to dull the senses before the morning recess.

No courtroom had *ever* smelled as lush and intriguing as the breeze wafting around this little Scottish cottage. Neither had the drawing studios at the art school.

Mr. Cromarty took the place beside Louise, the chains creaking as the swing dipped.

"Shall I show you the studio now, or would you like to finish that nap you started?"

All the useful pieces of Louise's mind had been flung 38,000 feet in the air, and they weren't floating back to earth in the right order. The lawyer part of her couldn't seem to connect with the art teacher part of her, and neither of those had quite hitched up to her body or her usual sense of organization.

A sensible woman would take a nap—or finish the nap she'd started.

"Would you sit with me for a few minutes, Mr. Cromarty?" Louise wanted his warmth, wanted that comfortable-in-his-own-skin vibe right by her side.

"This is a pretty place to bide," he said, ranging an arm along the back of the swing. "I have good memories of this cottage. I wrote my doctoral thesis here."

A yes, then. A friendly yes to her request for company.

He was Dr. Cromarty, PhD, but hadn't bothered with the academic title when introducing himself. More evidence that Liam Cromarty knew exactly who he was, and had nothing to prove to anybody.

Whereas Louise—

"Why the sigh, Miss Cameron?" He pushed off with the heel of his boot and set the swing in motion.

"I cannot recall being this tired since finals week my third year of law school," Louise said. "I think I've been tired for a long time, but that plane ride did me in." Or maybe she hadn't had anybody to sit with in years. "What's your PhD in?"

"Art history."

A rosy sense of good cheer took up residence in Louise's middle. Liam Cromarty liked art. How many guys liked art, much less made it their primary area of study?

"I like art too." Good to recall that. At one time, Louise had loved art with a stupid passion.

"Right—you're a potter."

Pot-ter. Once upon a time, Louise had been a *ceramic artist*. The hottest talent to hit the galleries in years, supposedly, though hot talent and galleries struck her as a contradiction in terms now.

"I've thrown some pots. I'd like to do more of that while I'm here." Louise would also like to rest her head on Liam Cromarty's shoulder, but snatched the last scintilla of dignity from her carry-on brain and resisted that temptation.

The wind died as the thunder rumbled yet closer.

"The studio's stocked and waiting for you, Miss Cameron. My cousin Morag works in ceramics, and if her own facilities ever come a cropper, the wheel and kiln here are her backup plan."

"Everybody needs a backup plan. What's a nice PhD like you doing driving tourists around old Scotia? Am I your backup plan?"

The first soft patter of rain hit green leaves, faded, then resurged into a steady downpour.

"You're a favor to my cousin Jeannie, with whom you did most of your corresponding. For the next two weeks I'm between terms, and I know my way around fairly well."

Louise had lost her way. With thousands of miles between her and a cookie-cutter apartment in nearby York, Pennsylvania, she could see that. What she could not fathom was why Scotland should feel so welcoming, irrespective of the man sitting next to her.

"I'll fall asleep if we stay out here much longer."

Mr. Cromarty was off the swing in one lithe movement. "Come along, then. I'll show you around, and you can catch forty winks."

CHAPTER TWO

Mr. Cromarty extended a hand to Louise, and she took it, though such was her fatigue that when she stood, she needed a moment to get her bearings. He kept her hand in his, until Louise was the one to let go.

The cottage was designed with recessed lighting that brightened up an interior the surrounding trees could have made gloomy. In the kitchen and dining area, which sat to the left of the front door, the floors were flagstone. To the right, the living room had polished oak floors, a fieldstone hearth along the inside wall, and picture windows looking out on the woods.

"The photos on the web site don't do this cottage justice," Louise said. "They don't show the trees, the skylights, the ferns, the books, or,"—the sense of homecoming welled again, higher this time—"*the kitty.*"

Mr. Cromarty left off opening drawers and cupboards in the kitchen.

"So this is where the damned hairy bugger has got off to. Please tell me you're not allergic?" He scooped up what had to be twenty pounds of long-haired black feline from the sofa, and from across the room, Louise heard a stentorian purr.

"I'm not allergic. I like cats." Robert had detested them. Louise suspected he'd been less than gentle with Blackstone when she hadn't been home to referee.

"There's a cat door in back," Mr. Cromarty said, "but I thought I'd locked it shut. Dougie won't be any bother, but I can take him home with me if you'd rather."

The cat booped Mr. Cromarty's chin with his head then turned golden eyes on Louise as if to say, "I saw him first."

"I can use the company," Louise said, stroking a hand over the cat's back. "His name's Dougie?"

"Black Douglas. He ought to be Black Shameless."

Another head boop. Mr. Cromarty loved his shameless cat, and the cat—if ever a cat were to admit such thing—loved Mr. Cromarty.

"Leave Dougie with me," Louise said. "I'm sure he'll find his way home when he's hungry enough."

"Starvation plagues him unceasingly."

Mr. Cromarty didn't turn loose of the cat, but kept him cradled in a purring, contented embrace as Louise was given a tour of the cottage. In addition to the kitchen/dining area and living room, the downstairs held a half bath and a small ceramic studio complete with fridge, kiln, shelves, tools, and a small plastic trash can for clay.

Upstairs was divided into a bedroom that felt like a treehouse—much of the ceiling was a skylight—and a study with computer and reference books. Both the study and the bedroom had floor-to-ceiling picture windows, and from the bedroom a placid river was visible through the trees.

"There's food in the fridge," Mr. Comarty said as they trooped downstairs. "The basics, and a few things Jeannie says are essentials. We can pick up anything else you need tomorrow. You've a charger for your phone and laptop?"

"I do, one for each." Jane and Dunstan had seen to that, and the requisite adapter plugs. "When shall we leave tomorrow?"

Louise had scheduled a trip to the Scottish National Portrait Gallery, a hike up Arthur's Seat, and a visit to Rosslyn Chapel, none of which would happen unless she was thoroughly rested.

"I'd like to get an early start," she added.

"We'll want to miss traffic, so there's not much point leaving before eight thirty a.m. Does that suit?"

They'd returned to the porch, where the eaves dripped damply, though the rain had either paused or moved on.

"I will probably sleep until then," Louise said, "which seems a shameful waste of a day in Scotland."

Mr. Cromarty shifted the cat to his other shoulder with the ease of a parent handling a sturdy baby.

"You take a nap, Miss Cameron. After an hour or two at most, get up and go for a walk. If you look in the desk drawer in the study, you'll find a map of the walking trails, and the one along the river is mostly level as far as the waterfall. Go for a ramble, check your e-mail—we're five hours ahead of the East Coast—and curl up with a book and a sandwich. That'll set you up for the rest of your stay."

Louise scratched the cat's chin, though that meant sharp claws dug into the shoulder of Mr. Cromarty's jacket.

"You've done this?" she asked. "Flown across the Atlantic?"

"Many times, though not as often in recent years. If you need me, my house is straight out the back, through the trees about fifty yards. You can't miss it, and the door's never locked."

Louise's apartment in York was locked and alarmed, though what would anybody steal? A lot of sketchbooks featuring portraits of her own feet, Robert's hands, or a sleeping Blackstone.

"Thanks, Mr. Cromarty. I'll expect you tomorrow at eight-thirty."

Louise meant to pluck the cat from his shoulder, but Dougie was a cat, and thus her efforts were resisted by virtue of several claws hooked deeply into Mr. Cromarty's lapel.

"Drat the beast," he muttered, trying to extricate the cat's claws one by one. Dougie, however, had no intention of parting with his owner, and grabbed on with his free paw just as the first paw was unfastened.

"Let me," Louise said. "You hold him, and I'll—"

She slid a hand between Mr. Cromarty's jacket and his chest, which was covered with a black T-shirt. The result was a few moments of tactile intimacy nobody—except perhaps the cat—had planned on.

Mr. Cromarty smelled delicious. Against the back of Louise's hand, he gave off an animal warmth, and this close he was pure, solid male. She was hit with a wave of stupidity—fatigue, female awareness of the man she touched, and bewilderment at the entire situation.

"Dougie, let go," Mr. Cromarty growled. "Bad kitties get no tuna fish."

Having destroyed Louise's composure and perhaps some of Mr. Comarty's, the cat turned up docile and cuddled against Louise's middle.

"Stay with Miss Cameron," he said, shaking a finger at the cat, "or I'll throw you in the river where the fishes can make sport of you. You can be our own local river monster."

The cat blinked and, if anything, purred more loudly as his owner thumped down the porch steps.

"Mr. Cromarty?"

He paused amid the rocks and bracken at the foot of the steps, a man whose looks would not substantially change for the rest of his life. Liam Cromarty wasn't exactly handsome, but he was attractive. Very attractive. Also patient, considerate, fond of cats, and interested in art.

"Miss Cameron?"

"Could you—? I mean, I don't know what's expected here. In Scotland. Between relative strangers. And you have to be honest if it's not appropriate. Could you call me Louise?"

"Liam," he said, without an instant's hesitation. His smile had nothing of the wolf, but it crinkled his blue eyes and lit up his face with a breathtaking warmth. "And I shall call you Louise."

* * *

"The American spinster stole your man," Liam informed Helen. She cocked her shaggy head, tongue lolling, but didn't leave her bed.

"We're getting old," Liam said, closing the door behind him. He'd taken the dog for a good hike before going to the airport, but the larger breeds tended to age sooner, and one walk a day was Helen's limit anymore.

"C'mon," Liam said. "Up with you. We're not quite decrepit, and the back porch awaits."

Helen got to her feet, shook her head hard enough to make her big ears flap, and obediently followed Liam through the house to the screened back porch. The rain had left the woods damp, fragrant, and sparkly with midday sun. Rather than go bounding off through the bushes, all Helen did was squat among the bracken and then commence sniffing a few rocks.

"I resent that Miss Cameron has borrowed my cat," Liam told the dog. "You don't appear to miss him."

Helen glanced his way and went back to her investigations. She was mostly deerhound, with some mastiff thrown in and perhaps a bear or two on the dam side.

Liam was debating whether to have lunch or grade the last of the term's papers when his phone rang.

Jeannie. He debated letting the call ring through to voice mail, but she'd simply keep calling and texting until he answered.

"She's here," Liam said, "and likely asleep by now, and yes, I changed the sheets last night." From flannel to cotton, a pattern of roses that smelled of the lavender sachets Jeannie stashed in the linen closet.

"Hello to you too, Liam," Morag said. "Jeannie's putting the baby down, so I'm using her phone. Did you know she and Harold have been fighting?"

"That doesn't mean they're getting a divorce," Liam said, gently, because Morag was angry in proportion to how badly she hurt, and lately she'd been very angry.

"You've not been married for a long time, Liam," Morag said. "There's fighting and there's fighting. Henry doesn't sleep through the night yet, and nobody fights fair when they're exhausted. What's the latest American like?"

The latest American was tall, pretty, and had a weakness for Scottish vowels of the male persuasion. She would like Liam's back porch, and probably like Helen, too.

"Seems a sensible sort, but then, lawyers often are. Thanks for kitting out the pot shop."

"If she wants more than the basics, send her to me. We'll throw mud together. Jeannie says to tell you Miss Cameron has been to art school."

"Bugger what Jeannie says." Bugger all of Liam's interfering relations, rooting about in his life like Helen on the scent of a rabbit. "Just because a woman has taken a class in throwing pots doesn't mean she'll fancy a fellow who's fascinated by brush work in Low Country Renaissance masters."

Though Miss Cameron—*Louise*—also liked cats. A fine quality in any woman.

"Jeannie wants to see you happy, Liam." Morag's scold was all the more effective for being uncharacteristically gentle.

"For the next two weeks, I'll burn up a fortune in gas, see all the sights we were dragged to repeatedly as children, and pretend yet another loch is the most beautiful scenery on earth." Moreover, Liam would be *cheerful* for those two weeks, because Jeannie had asked this of him. "Enough about my non-holidays. How are you, Morag?"

Liam could do a credible version of the older-cousin inquisition with Morag because he *was* older, and because she'd been away at university for most of the year following Karen's death.

"I'm fine."

Liam could picture the exact "I'm fine" smile Morag wore. Helen growled through such a smile when confronted with a small, male dog intent on taking liberties.

"Jeannie says you've lost weight, Morag."

A pause ensued, during which Morag might have been taking the phone to a more private location—or counting to ten.

"Jeannie is a mother," Morag said. "Their vision changes when they give birth, so everybody looks in need of a meal or three. I think she's fallen asleep with the little rotter, Liam."

Morag was asking a question, as best Morag knew how to ask anything of anybody.

"Don't let her sleep in the same bed as the baby, but before you kidnap Henry off to his crib, tell me how you're doing, Morag Colleen Cromarty."

"I hate you, you know."

"That well?"

"I'm goddamned lonely, Liam. I'm glad to be free of Dean, but I'm lonely. He was at least somebody to resent, and now…" Her voice dropped. "Jeannie said you went a little crazy when Karen died. I can't imagine being this lonely and grieving too. How did you stand it?"

Not well. Not well at all.

"Your vision becomes impaired," he said, as Helen's pale, plumed tail waved among the bracken like a flag of surrender. "You learn not to see very far behind you or in front of you. You do the next necessary thing, and time and pride eventually pull you up out of the ditch."

"I'm making the ugliest gnomes you've ever seen. Nasty little fellows that ought to bring exorbitant sums."

They were probably merry, fat, and cute. "Watch the drinking, love."

"No worries. Can't throw a decent pot when I'm blutered."

Then thank God for Morag's pottery wheel. "Tell Jeannie the American is fine, and I'll take good care of her."

"I'll tell her the American is a right terror, and this will be the longest two weeks of your life."

"Save me a gnome. Love you, More."

The line went dead.

Liam was something of a thorn in his family's side because he *told* them he loved them. Said the words often and in public, Scottish reticence be damned.

Helen's head lifted, her gaze turning toward the river. Down on the path along the bank, Miss Cameron went marching by.

"Sit," Liam said softly. "We have papers to grade, and we're too old to go chasing after tourists. Besides, she doesn't kiss men she's just met."

And for her scruples, Liam liked her all the more.

* * *

Robert Stiedenbeck, III, had wanted to remain friends with Louise.

"We're colleagues, too, aren't we, Lou?" he'd asked as he'd packed for New York. "We'll keep in touch, and you can read my stuff for me, the same as always. If you want to visit the Big Apple, our couch is always available."

Our couch. His and his Sweet Young Thing's.

Louise had watched him go, feeling as much relief as heartache. Robert had seemed like a good idea at the time, but he'd also reminded her of Dr. Allan Hellenbore, professor of studio arts, seduction, and ceramic forgery. Same friendly, self-mocking arrogance, same quick intellect coupled with an instinct for self-interest that boded ill for anybody else's dreams.

Louise could go for months without thinking of Allan Hellenbore. She'd learn not to think of Robert. Not to be angry at him, not to wonder what in the hell—

The first step toward not thinking about somebody was to not think of them.

"Rise and shine," Louise muttered to the cat plastered to her side. Dougie lifted his head, stared at her, and stretched to a magnificent length.

"My, what impressive claws you have," she said, dragging the cat onto her belly. Overhead, the skylight framed a leafy canopy, birds flitted, and morning sunshine poured across it all at a low angle.

While in Louise's lavender-scented bed, Dougie was a comforting, warm, rumbly weight.

"I've been here only a day, and already, I know I won't want to go back to York," Louise murmured. "This is not good, Cat. I don't want to teach drawing to a bunch of giggling children. They're either texting their weekend hookup, or convinced they're the next Michelangelo. I'm even more sure I don't want to go back into the courtroom."

That prospect loomed like "backup time," the sentence hanging over a convicted criminal's head if the conditions of parole weren't met. A taste of liberty, and then—a speeding ticket, a little too much to drink—wham, back in the hoosegow.

Dougie took to kneading the sheets.

"You are a good kitty. I like you. You must be hungry." Dougie wasn't a fat cat. He was simply big, all over big, and hairy. "I'll miss you when I leave, and how pathetic is that?"

"Hullo, the house!" a man's voice called.

Dougie sprang from the bed and disappeared into the hallway, tail up, a cat on a mission.

"Gimme a minute!" Louise bellowed back. The clock said 7:45, but perhaps Liam had brought more scones. The leftovers from yesterday were in the fridge, minus the chocolate chippers that had been Louise's dessert and snack.

Also her dinner. One of her dinners. The other had been a grilled cheese-on-rye sandwich.

She slipped into jeans and a T-shirt, then grabbed a flannel shirt for the sake of modesty and padded after the cat.

The guy standing in her kitchen was *not* Liam. "Who are you?"

Bonnie Prince Charlie's grandpa left off munching one of the cinnamon scones Louise had been saving for Liam. He was white-haired, tall, thick-chested, and wore a red plaid kilt along with boots, knee socks, and bright red T-shirt.

"You were fishing yesterday, weren't you?" Louise asked.

He'd been wearing plaid waders—the better to attract Scottish trout?—and singing something about rantin' and rovin'. Louise had stuck to the path and quietly passed by, and when she'd returned, he'd been gone.

"I might ask the same question, lass: Who are you? I see you've passed muster with ma' wee friend Dougie."

Dougie stropped himself against heavy boots, clearly comfortable with the intruder. Louise sensed no threat from the guy, no menace, though the cinnamon scone was rapidly becoming history.

"Did you find the butter?" she asked.

"Aye, thank you, and the coffee's on. I'm Uncle Donald. Welcome to Dunroamin Cottage. I expect you're Jeannie's latest American?" He passed her the box of scones, which held one plain and two raspberry.

Louise had never had an Uncle Donald. Now might be a fine time to acquire one. "If you made coffee, you're welcome to stay," she said. "Did you catch anything while you were fishing yesterday?"

"I'm in the river most days, though I seldom call it fishing. What brings you to Scotland?"

A need to see fairy lights at dusk, and find strange old fellows making coffee in the morning? The coffee maker hissed and gurgled, and a heavenly aroma filled the kitchen.

"I wanted to get away," Louise said, "and I've never been here before. Shall we sit?"

Uncle Donald put whole milk on the table and a bowl of white and brown lumps of sugar. Dougie sat before the fridge, switching his plume-y tail, until Uncle Donald took down a quarter-size green ceramic bowl from the cupboard and filled it with milk.

"The beasts train us, poor dumb creatures that we are," he said, passing Louise the milk and setting out two plates. "You Americans like your orange juice, am I right?"

"Please. Are all Scottish men so well trained?"

"I'm a bachelor," Uncle Donald said. "One learns to fend for oneself."

For an instant, blue eyes focused on Louise, not unkindly, but as if the statement had some significance she wasn't awake enough to figure out.

"Do you drink coffee?" she asked.

"Perish the notion. I drink tea, and whisky, of course." He produced a flask covered in green and blue plaid. "Shall you have a wee nip?"

Whisky in the fudge and whisky for breakfast. No wonder people loved Scotland. "No, thank you."

He tipped back the flask, his wee nip not so wee. "I do love a good island single malt. What's your name, Yank?"

Louise was torn between a sense of privacy invaded, and the novelty of having company for breakfast.

"Louise Cameron, attorney at law, sort of." She could go a-lawyering again if she had to, couldn't she?

"Camerons are thick on the ground here, though they haven't always been popular. Eat, child. Are you and Jeannie off to the city, then? Fine day to see the sights."

Louise dipped a corner of the raspberry scone in her coffee.

"Liam is taking me into Edinburgh today. We're supposed to see the portrait gallery, then tool out to Rosslyn Chapel, and finish with a climb up Arthur's Seat."

Another not-so-wee nip. "Busy folk, you Americans. Shall you put butter on that?" He nudged the butter dish to Louise's side of the table.

She nearly said, "Aye," such was the Scottish gravitational pull of Uncle Donald's company. "The butter here is good."

"The food here is good," he countered. "We don't go for those android crops you make in your laboratories. Our dairy is mostly organic, as is much of our produce. You must also try the whiskys, though Liam won't be much help in that regard."

"You're his uncle?"

"I'm the Cromarty uncle-at-large, more or less. You mustn't mind Liam."

Family was family the world over. Aunt Evangeline had probably said those same words about Louise to half the bachelors in Atlanta. *You mustn't mind Louise. She went to school Up Nawthe.*

"What does that mean, I mustn't mind Liam?" Louise liked Liam, right down to his t's, and d's, and the crow's-feet fanning from his eyes.

"We try to include him," Uncle Donald said, "but the boy's not very includable. Hasn't been since—"

A sharp rap on the door interrupted whatever confidence Uncle Donald had been about to inflict on Louise. Lawyers probably heard more dirty family laundry than therapists did, and she certainly didn't want to hear Liam Cromarty's.

She opened the door to find the man himself on her doorstep. The cat shot out between his legs, while Uncle Donald remained at the table, munching the last of Louise's raspberry scone.

"Uncle, what a surprise." Liam clearly wasn't pleased to see Donald, and neither was he surprised.

"Liam, good day to ye. Help yourself to a scone, and the coffee's hot."

Liam wore a kilt, another black T-shirt, and a wool jacket. The only resemblance between the two men, though, was size and blue eyes.

"I have an aunt just like Uncle Donald," Louise said, patting Liam's chest. "Every bit as presuming, though not half as likable. You might as well have some coffee. I'm not quite ready to leave."

"Liam doesn't eat meat," Uncle Donald observed as he dusted his fingers. "Makes him skinny and cranky, but a day in the city will do the boy good."

"At least I don't housebreak uninvited," Liam remarked, taking up Dougie's empty green bowl and running it under the tap. "You'll cost Jeannie her business one of these days, old man. Miss Cameron's a lawyer. She can sue you for unlawful entry and pilfering her scones."

Liam sounded more Scottish—"auld mon"—and he looked more Scottish in his kilt and boots. He smelled the same, though. Spicy, woodsy, delightful.

"Save me the last raspberry scone," Louise said, "and Uncle Donald, it was a pleasure to meet you—mostly."

With two Cromarty men in the kitchen, the space became significantly smaller. Louise took herself upstairs, grabbed a shower, finished dressing, and came down to find Liam alone, putting the last of the dishes away.

"You can relax," Louise said. "Uncle Donald hadn't really warmed up before you got here, and your deep, dark secrets are safe for now."

Liam draped a red plaid towel just so over the handle to the oven. "You have an aunt like him?"

"She has to let everybody know I graduated first in my law school class, and that business with art school was a funny little idea I picked up from the Yankees, bless their hearts."

Liam stared at the towel, his hands tucked into his armpits. "And every time she says it, you hurt a bit, but you've learned not to show it. I don't drink spirits."

Every time Aunt Evangeline dismissed four years of hard work and heartbreak as a silly little phase, Louise died inside. When Aunt Ev started in on *that awful man* and *the silly business about the pots*, Louise spent days in hell.

"Sobriety is a fine quality in the man who'll be driving me all over Scotland, Liam."

His shoulders relaxed, his hands returned to his sides. "I enjoy a good ale, and I've been known to have a glass of wine."

The topic was sensitive, though, and personal, so Louise changed the subject. "Do we pack lunch, or eat on the run?"

"We'll eat atop of Arthur's Seat, unless you have an objection to picnicking?"

Louise had not gone on a picnic for… she couldn't recall her last picnic. "No objection at all. Let me grab my jacket and purse, and last one to the car is a rotten egg."

When she joined Liam at the car, he held the door for her, and she climbed in, prepared to enjoy a day that combined art, architecture, exercise, and natural beauty.

Also some company, though who would have thought: Liam Cromarty, that Scottish male monument to relaxed confidence and easy grace, had deep, dark secrets after all.

* * *

Liam enjoyed art—sublime art, ridiculous art, functional art, art that struggled, art that failed, art that did both.

The greatest work of art ever conceived, however, was the human female.

He'd forgotten that.

Louise Cameron first thing in the morning was a different creature entirely from Louise striding around the busy airport terminal, Louise making pronouncements about whom she did and did not kiss, and Louise marching down the river trail.

Louise in the morning was sweet, a little creased around the edges, and intriguing. Liam wanted to kiss her, wanted to bury his hands in long skeins of dark red hair, wanted to sit her on the counter and learn the fit of their bodies.

Which, of course, he would not do. Spring was in the air, and he'd been forced into proximity with a pretty woman—who had artistic inclinations, didn't censure a man for avoiding spirits, and was punctual.

She came swinging down the cottage staircase at eight twenty a.m., dewy and neat in jeans, trainers, and a purple-and-green tie-dyed T-shirt. Her hair was coiled into a low bun held up by no means Liam could discern, and she appeared to be free of makeup—probably the secret to her punctuality.

"I've stashed the last two scones in my sporran," he said. "We can finish them off on the way to Edinburgh."

Louise opened the fridge and passed him four eggs.

"Hard-boiled," she said. "Woman does not live by carbs and fat alone, as tempting as the prospect might be—unless you're vegan?"

Damn Donald's big, presuming, well-intended mouth. "I eat eggs and dairy happily and in quantity." Liam had also been known to enjoy the occasional hapless fish when his body craved protein and the menu offered no vegetarian fare.

"My kinda guy," Louise said, tucking an orange into her purse. "Do we have water in the car?"

"We always have water in the car, trail mix and energy bars." Also a first aid kit, a pair of thermal sleeping bags, waterproof matches, and a pup tent, none of which Liam had ever used. "Do you want to practice driving?"

He'd surprised her—also himself, the Mercedes being less than a year old—but he'd pleased her too.

"How about if I take a day to get acclimated and watch the master in action?" she said. "I missed the countryside yesterday, and I don't want to make that mistake again today."

"The countryside is worth a look," Liam said, getting the door. "And you'll have plenty of opportunity to drive."

He, however, had seen the countryside between Perthshire and Edinburgh countless times. He had not seen a woman lick her fingers one by one, when she'd finished her scone.

"Are you happy, Liam?"

Americans. "I hardly know you, Louise." Probably the other half of why he'd thought—fleetingly—of kissing her. "Why would I answer such a personal question honestly?"

"It's only a personal question if the answer's no. I'm not happy either, and I don't enjoy admitting it."

Nobody had asked her to. "Sometimes contentment is the more reasonable goal. Why did you choose the portrait gallery over the National Gallery?"

She allowed him to change the subject, explaining that she wanted the more Scottish collection. Talk wandered to the various galleries in the Washington, DC, area, which were many and varied.

And she knew them well, including their most recent exhibitions.

"Edinburgh looks old," she said when Liam had wedged the Mercedes into a parking space. "But pretty-old, like your grandma. Not tired-old, like you feel after a bad breakup."

She said the damnedest things. Liam's phone buzzed, probably the call he was expecting from Stockholm.

"This is the less old part of town," Liam said. "The New Town, in fact, though if we're to hike Arthur's Seat, we'll nip over to the Old Town."

Liam dealt with his call when Louise took photos of the Walter Scott monument, and as they wandered in the direction of the gallery, he explained aspects of Edinburgh history every schoolboy took for granted. Louise paid attention to his ramblings and to their surroundings. More than once, she simply stood in the middle of the sidewalk, face upturned to the morning sun, eyes closed.

"Do you do that at home?" Liam asked when she opened her eyes. "Do you stop in the middle of the street and gather freckles?"

"I should do it at home. Freckles are where the angels kissed you."

"I suppose you kiss angels on first acquaintance?"

Louis smacked him gently on the arm, smacked him out of his bad mood, as Jeannie or Morag might have. Karen hadn't been a smacker, and she'd valued her complexion.

At the portrait gallery, the punctual, dainty, quasi-Yankee tourist disappeared, and a different woman entirely emerged: quiet, focused, capable of remaining still for long moments before a portrait or bust.

Unfortunately, Liam liked that woman—liked her too—and found himself again speculating about her kisses.

* * *

No wonder Scottish men could bebop around in skirts.

They knew *who they were*, knew where their people had set up camp thousands of years ago, knew where they'd stood as the Roman legions had trooped past along the coast, hundreds of feet below the lookouts, and knew where they'd watched as those same Romans had gone scampering back south, willing to leave "the last of the free" to their hills and lochs.

The Scots knew where their battles had been fought, knew who'd won, and who was still losing.

Liam shared local history with Louise as a conscientious host would, but after twenty minutes at the portrait gallery, Louise put her foot down.

"Turn off the history lecture, professor. I don't know what manner of art historian you are, but to me, the joy of a good painting is that it shows us the painter as well as the subject, and sometimes even the entire society in which the painter created. I'd rather spend a good long while with three interesting paintings, than whip by three galleries in the same time. Go read a newspaper or something. You don't have to babysit me."

Liam's chin came up in such a manner that had Louise been a Roman, she would have started her southerly scamper at a dead gallop.

"I have a wee cousin, Louise. Henry cries, he wets, he burps, he does more objectionable things. Him, I babysit. This is a gallery. Here, I frolic."

Liam had a somber version of frolicking, standing before some paintings as if he could hear them, smell them, and slip through time to see the artist applying the paint to the canvas. One portrait in particular, of a brown-haired fellow in plain late-Georgian attire, held his attention longer than any other.

"Who's that?" Louise asked.

"Robert Burns."

"The Auld Lang Syne guy?"

He gave her a look that said clearly, *God spare me from American ignorance.*

"The very one. Shoo. This is an interesting painting. I'm busy. Be off with you."

Louise bopped him on the arm—he'd smiled at her the first time she'd done it, a sweet, surprised, genuine smile—and moved off to some magnificent royal portraits.

There was probably no explaining Scotsmen, but by God, they could paint. The gallery also had a number of busts, and those Louise found as fascinating as the paintings.

"We're behind schedule," Liam informed her when she'd finally reached the limit of what she could absorb. "Rosslyn Chapel closes at five p.m. this time of year, and you don't want to rush your visit. I propose we see the chapel and then take our walk up Arthur's Seat."

"Why didn't you tell me I was running over?" A schedule was important. Law school had taught Louise that, and private practice had taught it to her all over again. Even an art teacher had to be organized, or papers never got graded, office hours weren't kept—

Liam looked off, his expression vintage stoic-unreadable-Scot as a breeze flapped his kilt around knees that also managed to look stoic.

"You were happy, Louise. I didn't want to intrude."

She had been happy. Utterly absorbed by symbolism, brushwork, technique, palette, conventions, innovations, politics, images, noses, costumes—captivated by art in a way that renewed and exhilarated even as it drained.

And Liam had *noticed* that she was happy. Louise wished *he* could be happy, and not simply content.

She kissed his cheek and resisted the urge to hug him.

"Thank you, Liam. I had a wonderful morning. Let's grab a bite, hit the chapel, then do Arthur's Seat."

His smile was shy and a little bewildered. "Right. *Grab* a bite, *hit* the chapel, and *do* Arthur's Seat. Brilliant."

CHAPTER THREE

Rosslyn Chapel was a cathedral in miniature, a gem of fifteenth-century extravagance intended to ensure the St. Clair family a warm welcome in heaven. Thanks to well-timed preservation work and mention in a little book by Dan Brown, the chapel also welcomed tens of thousands of visitors every year.

"Who's that?" Louise asked when they'd paid their fare and crossed onto the green surrounding the building.

Liam saw nobody but— "That is the chapel cat. I don't know his name."

"Even the chapels have kitties in Scotland. Do you know how lucky you are?"

Louise picked up the cat, a well-fed black beast who, apparently sensible of the relationship between tourist revenue and his diet, began to purr.

The cat also gave Liam a "she likes me best" look.

Dougie had worn the same expression, last Liam had seen him. "I'll be in the building, Louise. No photos allowed inside."

Without setting the cat down, Louise passed him her cell phone. "My first photo in Scotland, and I'm with a handsome, dark-haired man of few words. If you wouldn't mind?"

Liam had held the camera up to his eye before he realized he'd been teased. "Shall I leave that gargoyle perched on your head?"

"You will do exactly as you please, Liam Cromarty."

He positioned the shot so the blue Scottish sky and the massive stone of the chapel—no gargoyle—formed the backdrop to an image of a smiling woman and a smug cat. The composition was perfect, the sort of balance that often came from careful contrivance, while the content was anything but contrived.

Before Liam handed the phone back, he e-mailed himself a copy of the photo. An art appreciation class could learn a lot from it.

While Louise read every bit of literature inside the chapel, and peered at length at stonework so delicate as to defy modern comprehension, Liam studied *her*.

The lady did nice things for a pair of worn jeans, and she did nicer things for Liam's mood. She had the knack of challenging without threatening, of offering insights instead of hurling them at him, cousin-style.

Rather than intrude on her further acquaintance with the chapel, Liam went outside, found a sunny bench, followed his phone call from Stockholm with a text to Copenhagen, and then took out the latest of the many art periodicals he tried to keep up with.

He was slogging through another attempt by Robert Stiedenbeck, III, to be profound and witty on the subject of fur as symbolism in American colonial portraiture when Louise joined him on the bench.

"I suppose you've seen the chapel a dozen times?" she asked.

"At least, and I'll see it a dozen more. When I teach in Edinburgh, we bring the class here. The chapel makes an excellent starting point for discussions of the economics of art, and how art can make a different contribution to society as that society changes over centuries."

"They stabled horses in there during the Reformation," Louise said as the cat leaped onto the bench. "Horses, Liam. One swift kick from a cranky mare, and wham, a detail on a carving somebody labored two years to create could have been gone."

Americans had had a revolution and a civil war, but without the oppression of a state religion, they were baffled by the complexity and violence of the Reformation.

The cat walked right into Louise's lap, with the same casual dignity as old ladies walked onto the ferry at the conclusion of an afternoon's shopping.

Liam offered the cat a scratch to the nape of its neck. "Fortunately, the mares were either equine Papists or more interested in their hay than architecture. What is it with you and cats?"

"Have you ever been to Georgia?"

"I have. Friendly place." And the food, holy God, the food… Fried heaven, even for a vegetarian, though the accent was baffling.

"I grew up there. Everybody's nice, but nobody's real, and then,"—she cradled the cat against her shoulder—"they can slice you to ribbons, all the while blessing your heart, darlin', and you poor thang, and that is such a shameing. I'm convinced the mixed message was invented by women of the American South."

"Family can be a trial." Liam had the sense Louise's family was worse than that. They were an ongoing affliction that bewildered her and wouldn't go away, like persistent grief.

"I grew up with cats," she said. "Cats are honest. If they don't want you to pick them up, they hiss and scratch. I love them for that. Love that they are simply what they appear to be, and if they enjoy your company, they are honest about that too."

Liam enjoyed Louise's company. He ought not. She wasn't precisely reserved, though she wasn't quite friendly either.

"Georgia is far away," Liam said, closing the periodical. "Family often means well as they're wreaking their havoc, and if you're lucky, they find somebody else to plague with their good intentions before you've committed any hanging felonies. Have you seen enough?"

Louise set the cat on the ground, and the beast went strutting off to its next diplomatic mission for the Scottish tourist industry.

"Your family was hard on you?" Louise asked.

She was a perceptive woman, so Liam gave her a version of the truth.

"I went through a bad patch a few years back. One of those bad breakups you mentioned earlier, followed by a bit too much brooding for a bit too long. They worried."

If Louise regarded that as an invitation to pry, Liam would have only himself to blame, because he never disclosed even that much. He'd done a bit too much drinking, too.

She picked up his magazine, a quarterly journal useful for inducing sleep or lining Dougie's litter box. Liam intended to cancel his subscription, but hadn't got 'round to it.

"You seem to have found your balance now," Louise said. "You read this stuff?"

"I read the abstracts. Somebody needs to teach most academics how to write. The article I attempted was worse than usual, though the learned Dr. Stiedenback will cite it at every lecture he gives for the next three years."

Louise made a face, as if the milk had turned. "You know him? This is an American journal."

"The art world is small, especially the gallery art world." And that world was the last topic Liam wanted to discuss with Louise Cameron. "Do you ever visit those people in Georgia?"

"Every other Christmas. They tsk-tsk over all the boyfriends I don't bring along, cluck about the New Year being full of new opportunities, and tell me I'm nothing but skin and bones."

Well, no actually, she wasn't. "They're of Scottish descent, then?"

Ah, a smile. At last another smile. Part of Liam had been waiting hours to see that smile, and now the image he beheld—pretty chapel, pretty spring day, pretty lady—went from well composed to lovely.

"You're hilarious, Liam Cromarty. As a matter of fact, they are Scottish on my father's side. Mom's DAR royalty—Daughters of the American Revolution— and related to Robert E. Lee, too. Daddy is the reason my sisters and I ended up with middle names like Mavis, Fiona, and Ainsley."

"Good names." Beautiful names. "Shall we head back to town? The temperature will drop as the sun sets, and Arthur's Seat can be windy."

Louise passed him the periodical and stood. "You really think that Professor Stiedenbeck doesn't write well?"

Odd question, but at least she wasn't interrogating Liam about his family.

"Somebody has taken pity on the bastard and assigned him a decent editor this time around, but he offers nothing original and takes a long-winded, self-important time to do it. Not very professional of me, but I imagine he's the sort who lectures his lovers into a coma before he gets on with the business, and then doesn't deliver much of a finish."

Lovely became transcendent as Louise fought valiantly against Liam's unprofessional humor and lost, heartily, at length, in happy, loud peals. She was still snickering when they got back to the car, and Liam was smiling simply because he'd made her laugh.

"Cromarty, please don't ever become an art critic," she said, opening a bottle of Highland Spring. "With analysis like that, you will develop a following wide enough to end the career of anybody you take into dislike."

Liam pulled out of the car park, and when Louise offered him a sip from the bottle, he politely declined.

* * *

Long-dormant powers of observation and analysis stirred inside Louise as she and Liam trekked up the eight-hundred-foot hill flanking Edinburgh to the southeast. The views were lovely, of course, but the terrain, like what she'd seen of Perthshire, wasn't much different from Maryland between the Appalachians and the Chesapeake shores.

And yet...

"I see differently here," Louise said as they stood aside to let an older couple coming down the slope pass them. "I'm noting the details, the colors, the relationships, the geometry. Maybe it's the light."

"Maybe you're on holiday," Liam countered, starting up the trail. "You got a good night's sleep, you're in different surrounds, and you're paying attention. One of the advantages of travel."

Louise paid attention to *him*, and not only because from a three-hundred-word abstract, he'd described Robert Stiedenbeck, III, exactly.

"Men move differently in kilts," Louise said, scrambling up a set of natural rock steps. "More freely. It's attractive."

Even the older guys with their walking sticks and stolid ladies at their sides moved with a certain assurance, but then, so did many of the unkilted men.

And all of the ladies.

"I was hoping I'd hate it here," Louise said, because clearly, Liam wouldn't dignify her comment about the kilts with a reply. "I'm not hating it."

"Hating is a lot of effort. Mind your step."

Liam needed to work on his charm, but he could hike the hell out of a Scottish hill.

"There are no guardrails here," Louise said, taking Liam's proffered hand to negotiate another natural incline. "No signs all over the place. Climb at Your Own Risk, or No Littering, or All Dogs Must Be on a Leash, or Scoop Your Poop."

No litter either. Nobody taking stupid risks.

Liam tugged her over a scattering of loose rock. "Sounds like a lot of noise and blather. How could you see the pretty landscape for all those lectures and scolds?"

Liam's question brought them to a stretch of gently rising grassy slope.

"Stop, please," Louise said, keeping hold of Liam's hand lest he conquer the summit on the strength of forward momentum alone.

He obliged as a quartet of teenagers went giggling and flirting past. "You're in need of a rest?"

"How could I see the pretty landscape for all those lectures and scolds?" Liam's words caught in Louise's throat as she repeated them. "Lectures about posture, deportment, the family name. Lectures about appearance, the right people. Lectures delivered with the arch of an eyebrow or a serving of pecan pie." Her breathing hitched, as if her lungs had been squeezed by a giant, familial hand. "Crap and a half, I thought I was done with all this."

Liam didn't drop her hand, and his grip was reassuringly warm. "Has your family come to call?"

He was quick—the Scots would call him canny—and his gaze was kind.

Louise managed a nod. "Anxiety along with them. I almost never have these episodes anymore. Damn."

She'd learned to breathe through the dread, to count her breaths instead of hoard them. She didn't have panic attacks. She had *episodes*, or—Auntie Ev had of course chimed in—*little spells*.

"Let's sit, shall we?" Liam suggested. The trail was flanked by boulders and rocky outcroppings in spots. He drew Louise over to one, and she sank against it. Liam came down beside her, right immediately beside her.

And he kept her hand in his.

"I'm sorry," Louise said, while the predictable elephant tried to sit on her chest. "New places, schedule whacked. Should have been more careful." Mention of Robert, when he was supposed to be thousands of miles away, lecturing another, younger, more confident woman into a coma, probably hadn't helped either.

Liam rubbed his thumb back and forth across Louise's knuckles. "You should be *less* careful. Enough new places and pretty views, and you'll get your heart back, but that takes time."

And courage. "You speak from experience?"

His thumb slowed. A dog that looked like Irish wolfhound-lite sniffed at Liam's knee, then went trotting off toward the top of the hill.

"I speak from experience, and from hope. Bad things happen, but then there are friendly dogs, beautiful portraits, delicious curries, and lovely views. There's wee Henry, whom I will spoil shamelessly exactly as I do his cousins. There's meaningful work, and a good sturdy piece of granite to oblige us when we're a bit winded."

A bit winded. Louise dropped her forehead to Liam's shoulder, as the certainty that all creation faced imminent doom faded, replaced by a simple lump in her throat.

"Were you a bit winded, after your bad breakup?" she asked.

"I was flat knackered, but I'd already been going too hard and too fast for too long."

"I've left the profession that was supposed to be my salvation," Louise said. "I've moved, ditched a relationship that wasn't right, and I have no idea where I'm going." And she'd been going at the lawyer stuff too hard and too fast for the five longest years in the history of lawyering, too. Trying to build a practice, trying to be a solid partner to Jane, who'd been born quoting *Marbury v. Madison*.

Liam's arm came around Louise's shoulders in a bracing squeeze. "Catch your breath, and we'll take the last part slowly. The hill isn't going anywhere, and we still have some light."

For one more moment, Louise had the blessed pleasure of Liam's hand in hers and his arm around her shoulders in a friendly hug. Then he stood, though he remained beside her.

Louise gave herself the space of three more slow, medium breaths—deep breaths could lead to hyperventilation—then got to her feet.

"I'm not going back to Georgia for Christmas," she announced. "Not this year, maybe not ever. Travel at the holidays is crazy, and I can see my sisters anytime." Especially now that her life wasn't ruled by the almighty court docket—though the academic calendar could be just as tyrannical.

"Onward, then," Liam said.

He had the knack of companionship, of neither leading nor following, but staying mostly at Louise's side. When the trail narrowed, he might go first, or Louise might. They didn't need to talk about who led or who followed or which fork to take when they faced a choice.

Because the afternoon was well advanced, the very top of the hill was mostly deserted. They passed the occasional couple or family on a picnic blanket, or a lone walker contemplating a view, but at the highest, rockiest point, they had the hill to themselves.

The North Sea glistened off to the northeast, while beyond Edinburgh, green countryside stretched inland around the Pentland Hills. Louise got out her phone, wanting to capture the memory of a wonderful day.

Despite the visit from her relatives.

"You're smiling," Liam said. "Shall I take a photo?"

"Please, and try not to put any gargoyles in my hair."

The same big, wire-haired dog came sniffing up the rocks, only this time his examination of Liam's knee was cursory. As Liam fiddled with the phone, the dog came panting to Louise's side.

"You smell the chapel kitty," Louise said, offering her hand for inspection. The dog licked her wrist, then took a seat at her feet as if photobombing was all part of the service, ma'am.

"The local Scottish Tourism Board representative wants his picture taken," Liam said as the camera clicked. "I expect the chapel cat sent him. You might smile now, Louise. Scottish deerhounds can be particular about the company they keep."

Louise smiled, because *she* was particular about the company she kept. No more Roberts—he had been a weak moment brought on by a career transition and a sexual drought—and no more pecan pie topped with mixed messages.

For the next two weeks her company would be Scotland and Dougie.

Also Liam Cromarty.

"I think I'll get a dog," she said. "A nice big, friendly dog." Blackstone would have to adjust, or join Jane and Dunstan's practice.

"I like dogs," Liam replied, as the camera clicked again. The breeze whipped his dark hair every which way, but his concentration as he tapped the screen was unwavering.

Down the hill, somebody whistled, and the deerhound trotted off.

"Your turn," Louise said, taking the phone from him. "Think Scottish thoughts."

"Just for that, I'll introduce you to tablet," Liam said, shifting so the wind blew his hair back, not into his eyes. "Or Jeannie's whisky brownies."

"You're talking to a Southern woman, Cromarty. Don't make me get out my bourbon cake recipe."

Viewing him through the camera lens, Louise had to both look and see. What aspect of this guy belonged in his portrait? What would those painters whose works hung in the gallery do with this subject?

Louise shifted the angle, so wide blue sky got honorable mention, along with the cairn of red-brown rocks topping the summit. The sea shone behind the hill, a flat, silver mirror saying farewell to the late-day sun.

And yet the kilted man standing off-center in the frame dominated the image easily.

"What's tablet?" Louise asked.

Just as she hit the shutter button, Liam smiled. Not a Scottish Tourism Board grin, not a pained male, "for God's sake, get it over with" smile.

"You would probably call tablet fudge," he said, with a hint of a challenge. "Sort of a blend of sweetened condensed milk and butter. The perfect treat to tide you over until supper, and I have some in my sporran."

Louise took a second shot of that slight, diabolical smile, but the fiend had dangled a lure her blood sugar couldn't resist. She put her phone away.

"What do I have to do to get some of this magical treat?" she asked.

They were alone at the top of Arthur's Seat, the light would soon fade, and Louise did not want to leave. The views were magnificent, and the climb—and the company—had done her good.

Liam dug in his sporran and passed her a bite-sized square the color of turbinado sugar.

"What you must do to earn this treat, Louise Cameron, is enjoy it."

The texture was perfect, between fudge and hard frosting, the sweetness underlain with the richness of cream. Hot, strong coffee would hold up to such a delectable morsel.

"This stuff ought to come with a gym membership," Louise said. "Chunky Monkey pales by comparison. You aren't having any?"

"My treat," Liam said, brushing a loose strand of hair back from her jaw, "is that right at this moment, you're happy. Tablet is not as delectable as the smile you're wearing, Miss Cameron."

On that unexpected bit of gallantry, he moved off down the incline.

Louise finished her tablet, munching slowly, letting the pleasure dissolve on her tongue as the sun sank lower and the sea gleamed on the horizon.

"I'm happy," she whispered, letting the realization replace all the anxious, dark, doubting feelings she often carried around inside. More baggage than she realized, heavier than she'd known. She lifted her arms to the sky, not caring if Liam was watching.

I'm happy.

When she'd clambered down to the path, she fell in beside Liam, content to walk beside him all the way back to the car park. The day had been magical, and some of the magic clung to her, even as she wondered:

What would it take for Liam to be happy too?

* * *

A prediction of rain saved Liam's sanity, for yesterday's frolics had about done him in. He took himself down the path to the cottage, intent on confirming with Louise that she'd not need her driver for the day.

Honesty compelled Liam to admit that Louise Cameron's *mouth*—a perfectly mundane arrangement of two lips—had about done him in. Her mouth had moods— thoughtful, determined, merry, frustrated. He'd taken to studying her mouth when he ought to have been studying portraits of old Rabbie Burns or Mad King George.

Louise was leaving in less than two weeks, but the image of her smiling atop Arthur's Seat would linger in Liam's memory long after her departure. More excellent composition, which he'd e-mailed to himself, but he'd probably not share those photos with his classes.

He knocked on the front door of the cottage, and nobody answered. From the base of the picture window, Dougie blinked up at him.

"I brought cat food," Liam informed his pet. "Though I suspect you've wheedled cheese and worse from the lady."

Dougie replied with a squint—a self-satisfied squint.

The door was unlocked, practically guaranteeing another visit from Uncle Donald. "Anybody home?" Liam called as he walked into the kitchen.

Perhaps Uncle Donald had kidnapped Louise for a spot of fishing. She had Liam's cell phone number, and might have called if her plans—

Somebody was down the hall in the studio, humming along to the strains of "Caledonia."

Bless the rainy forecast. Liam set the can of gourmet cat food on the kitchen counter, slung his damp jacket around the back of a chair, and eased down the hall.

Louise sat before the pottery wheel, a small column of wet, reddish clay rotating slowly between her hands. Liam's reaction was immediate, erotic, and inconvenient as hell.

He was going daft. First her mouth, then her hands. She pressed her thumbs into the top of the column, creating the beginnings of a dished shape, then continued to press, so the column developed a hollow interior.

Just like Liam's mind. Arousal, visual pleasure, consternation, and surprise rocketed about inside him, but nothing as coherent as an actual thought.

"I know you're there, Liam," Louise said as the clay became a vase. "I thought I heard the door, and I can smell your aftershave. You're allowed to watch. I'm not one of those artists who throws mud at someone who interrupts her work."

From the CD player, Dougie MacLean—*such* a helpful fellow—sang gently about kisses, love, and going home.

"Wouldn't fiddle music be easier to work to?" Liam asked, leaning on the doorjamb. "There's a Paul Anderson album in that stack that's breathtaking."

Everything Paul Anderson recorded was breathtaking.

Louise used the back of her wrist to scratch her chin and got a daub of wet clay on her jaw.

"I'll listen to them all before I leave, possibly before the day's done. The forecast said rain for most of the day."

And thunder and lightning behind Liam's sporran, apparently. For years he'd not been plagued with unforeseen arousal, with much of any arousal. His equipment functioned, he made sure of that from time to time, but Louise with her wet hands and her hair in a haphazard topknot had ambushed him.

"If you want to spend the day here, I have plenty of work to do," Liam said. "Papers to read, lecture notes to prepare. If you need anything, you have only to—"

"I need a hard-boiled egg or two and a cup of coffee."

Liam nearly told her, as he would have told any sister, cousin, or other presuming female, to get it herself or at least say please, but Louise hadn't looked up from her project. She bent closer to the wheel, shaping the vase into a taller column, gently, gently, then spreading the base with the same deft, sure movements.

She's happy. She was once again happy.

"You've done this a lot," Liam said. Louise did it well, too. Her expertise was evident in her focus and in the results of her efforts. Some people had the gift of creating art directly with their hands—no brushes, knitting needles, or musical instruments required. They had art—vision, texture, composition—in their very touch.

Louise apparently owned that gift, an ability that went beyond talent to the very nature of the beast doing the creation.

"Used to stay up all night, throwing and re-throwing the same clay. If clay worked for God, why not for a high school kid dragging around thirty extra pounds in all the wrong places?"

More self-disclosure, or another nod to the Georgia pecan pie mafia. "I'll fetch you an egg and a cup of tea."

"I asked for—damn it to hell and back. I'll need all day to learn this wheel. I asked for coffee."

"I don't know how to work that fancy machine," Liam said, and his ability to read directions was none too reliable at the moment. The smudge on Louise's chin was driving him 'round the bend. "Jeannie bought the coffee maker for a couple of German engineers who visited over the winter."

Then too, tea might steady Liam's nerves.

Without looking up, Louise smiled at her vase and let it pirouette on the wheel for a few rotations, delicacy and dirt dancing together. Then she demolished it, smushing it back onto the wheel with both hands so a formless lump of wet mud twirled off-center where art had been.

"Tea then," she said, using a tool that resembled a wire garrote to free the clay from the wheel. "And some of that tablet stuff you keep in your man purse."

"Sporran," Liam muttered, leaving the lady to her mud. He considered stopping off in the loo, he was that randy, but turned his thoughts to making tea, peeling three hard-boiled eggs, and slicing some cheddar made on the Isle of Mull—island cows were happy cows, according to Jeannie.

The tablet, he left in his sporran, for now.

"Breakfast," he said, setting a tray on the studio's work table a few minutes later. On the CD player, Mr. MacLean had mercifully switched to a pair of fiddles waltzing along in slow harmony.

"All I need is a bite," Louise muttered, leaning far enough forward that a loose hank of hair dropped forward over her shoulder.

An inch more forward and that hair would hit the wheel, which was arguably dangerous and certainly messy. Liam caught the errant lock and tucked it back among its mates.

"Thanks," Louise said, coaxing the clay upward. "This clay acts like it's cold, but it's not. We're having a discussion, the clay and I, or maybe an argument."

Liam held Louise's mug of tea up to her mouth. She took a sip, peering at him over the rim. The smudge of clay on her chin was drying to pale dust, and he wanted to brush it off so badly his fingers itched.

"A bite of egg?" he asked.

"I see you put salt on the tray. I like a sprinkle of salt on mine, please, but just a sprinkle."

As the clay twirled endlessly on the wheel, Liam suffered the torture of feeding the artist by hand. She nibbled delicately from his fingers, the intimacy endurable only because Louise was apparently oblivious to it.

Her attention had been seduced by a lump of wet clay, while Liam eyed the clock and wished the call he expected from Ankara would come in.

Though the image of Louise and the chapel cat had become his phone's wallpaper. Not very smart, that.

"You're an art historian," Louise said as a lovely fluted bowl was obliterated on the spinning surface. "Are you also an artist? I'll teach you to throw in return for driving lessons."

"I dabble with a sketch pad, but I haven't any real talent." Karen had assured Liam of that, but only in recent years had he ignored her laughing assessment and drawn anyway. "Would you like more egg?"

"Cheese first," she said. "I can smell it even in here. I love cheese."

"What happened to the thirty extra pounds?" Liam asked. Louise had found good homes for some of those pounds, in all the right places.

"My older brother got me a horse. Six months of practically living at the barn, and no more thirty extra pounds. I was mostly out of shape, sitting at the wheel by the hour when I wasn't sitting in classes at school, or sitting at my desk doing homework—"

Liam held the lightly salted egg up to Louise's mouth. She took a bite, then another.

"What happened to the horse?" he asked, mostly out of desperation.

"When I went to college, my parents gave me the choice of selling the horse or passing him along to my sister. I went off to school, and by Christmas, Bobo had been sold. My mother claimed my sister lost interest. My sister claimed Mom wouldn't drive her out to the barn."

Liam held up the egg again, and Louise's attention shifted from what had possibly been the beginning of a teapot to the food.

Liam didn't think. He let protectiveness, sexual arousal, and a need for her to not ignore him drive his actions. When Louise turned toward the half an egg

Liam held, instead of the egg he gave her a kiss.

"To hell with Georgia, Louise. If you were happy at the horse barn, sign up for lessons again. You're happy throwing. Set up your studio again. Teach other people to throw. Finish that art degree."

She remained right where she was, her mouth an inch from Liam's.

"I did." She kissed him back, then resumed tormenting her clay, as if people kissed in the course of discussion with her all the time. "I got the damned degree, a lot of good it did me. Tea?"

This art degree had made her unhappy, or perhaps art degrees didn't go well with pecan pie and controlling parents.

While lawyering hadn't gone well for Louise?

"Losing that weight, learning to ride, gave you strength your family wasn't accustomed to seeing in you," Liam said.

"Growing four more inches didn't hurt either," Louise replied, scraping the clay off the wheel. This time she shut the wheel off, so it spun gradually to a halt. "Your tea will get cold, Liam."

She picked up his cup in her wet, muddy hands and held it up to this mouth. He drank despite the incongruous scents of wet clay and roses blending with an understated Darjeeling he'd found in Edinburgh.

"I didn't mean to interrupt your work," Liam said. "You'll want to converse with your clay, and I'm sure—"

She took a drink of his tea. "I need to think about the clay. I've thought about something else, too, though. I've thought about taking you to bed."

CHAPTER FOUR

Scottish men were supposed to be hot, fun, and emotionally unavailable. Liam wasn't exactly fun, and he ignored his own sex appeal so thoroughly Louise might have blinked and missed it.

But emotionally, he paid attention. He listened, he saw, he thought about the information he took in. Careful he might be, also shy, reticent, and probably snake-bit—he'd mentioned a bad breakup—but he was emotionally more present than any guy Louise had spent time with since, well, Bobo.

Louise had thought about Liam Cromarty all night, just as, long ago, she might have imagined the last piece of pecan pie in the pantry. What the hell good was being on the rebound if she let the only guy to hold her attention in years go hiking out of her life without even letting him know she wanted to peek under his kilt?

"I have a theory," Liam said, setting his tea cup down in the precise middle of its saucer. "The standard wisdom is that American girls are easy."

He leaned back against the heavy worktable, looking like a relaxed, kilted cover for a men's magazine, right down to drinking his tea from a cup with a saucer under it.

"I'm not a girl." Nor was Louise in the mood for a morality lecture. "If you're not inclined, professor, a simple 'no thank you, pass the salt,' will do. I'm interested, I'm not easy." When nobody asked, a woman had no opportunity to *be* easy.

"Louise Cameron, I have noticed that you are no longer a girl."

Louise got up to wash her hands, the better to turn her back on Liam's rejection.

"I have noticed," Liam went on, "that you are an intelligent, interesting woman to whom I am attracted. You're also quite pretty, but a man never knows if he's supposed to mention a woman's appearance."

And next would come… the *but*. Liam would walk out the door, and Louise would never see him again. Some other handsome, smiling Cromarty would appear in a different vehicle, to do some Nessie-spotting or tour the nearest whisky distillery with her.

Louise resisted the urge to flick water at Liam. She instead did a very thorough job of washing the mud from her hands.

"I've never invited a guy into my bed before, Liam Cromarty. I don't expect I'll make a habit of it."

Because guys like him didn't come along very often. Not in her life. Louise got the slick, smart, dishonest kind instead. The users who never paid a price for their lack of honor and were proud of their guile.

The bow that held Louise's smock up came undone as she turned off the tap.

"You don't kiss strangers, Louise. I've long since outgrown any interest in disporting with easy women."

Liam spoke directly against Louise's bare nape, a stern, talking kiss that sent a lovely shiver through her. He'd taken off his leather purse thing, which he usually wore front and center over his kilt. His arousal was front and center now, snugged against Louise's backside.

"I like you, Liam. I respect you. I also desire you." More than that, Louise *trusted* him. He'd never casually assume she'd provide free editorial services for his stupid, stilted articles while he packed up to move in with another woman.

Another warm, lingering kiss, this one to the juncture of Louise's shoulder and her neck.

"I'm out of practice, Louise, but I like you and I respect you, too."

And holy God, could Liam use his mouth. He tasted, he teased, he nibbled, he bit Louise's earlobe *just right*, he slid his hands around her middle, and Louise would have cheerfully put the work table to use despite a lovely bed available on the next floor up.

"If you'll put away the clay," Liam said, patting her bottom, "I'll feed the cat and lock the door. Uncle Donald is ever fond of the sneak attack."

Louise managed a nod, grateful for a few minutes to compose herself—and to anticipate the rest of the morning in bed with Liam.

* * *

As Liam locked *and* dead-bolted the front, back, and side doors, he inventoried his internal security system, looking for panic, dread, second thoughts, anything that suggested intimacy with Louise Cameron was a bad idea.

"It's a messy idea," he told Dougie as he spooned wet food into the green bowl. "A complicated idea. Also irresistible."

Liam petted the cat, who went noisily and enthusiastically facedown into the dish of food.

"Maybe that's why I want to give it a go," he said softly. "One small ocean will limit my folly to two weeks fondly remembered."

He'd spoken the truth, though. He liked Louise and respected her. A lot. Far more than he'd liked the several encounters he'd allowed himself since Karen's death.

Louise had good timing, among her many other fine qualities.

"If she'd left the overtures to me," Liam said, "I'd have been putting her on that plane in two weeks, wondering what might have been and kicking myself for not—"

Louise came striding into the kitchen. "I fed Dougie before I got started this morning. He'll be sleeping off a tuna drunk, and that's a good thing." She kept coming across the kitchen, until she was smack up against Liam, her arms twined around his neck. "You never did tell me your theory."

Liam's theory was they should go upstairs immediately. "What theory?"

"About American women being easy."

That theory. "American women aren't any easier than any other variety of women," Liam said, as Louise led him down the hallway. "But American men are lazy, inconsiderate, incompetent louts. Their women get lonely and restless, and then some handsome, charming fellow sashays by while the lady's on her holiday—we need my sporran."

"And here I was hoping you'd lose the kilt."

Liam looked down at his oldest, plain black work kilt. The one he'd worn for the marathon writing sessions on his dissertation.

"I'm quite partial to this kilt."

"I meant, *take it off*, Liam." Louise swayed up the stairs ahead of him, a delectable sight in black yoga pants and a man's plain white T-shirt. Clay smudged the hem over one hip, and Liam would have bet his autographed first edition of Janson's *"History of Art"* that Louise wasn't wearing a bra.

He wanted to sketch her, smudges and all; wanted to see her throw pots naked; wanted to—fetch his sporran. When Liam got upstairs, Louise stood fully clothed by one of the picture windows, looking out on damp green woods.

"Good," Liam said. "I want to undress you. I want to take down your hair, want to—what?"

"Now you turn up loquacious and take-charge? What if I want to undress you first?"

In the midst of the rainy woods, the sun shone in Liam's heart, and quite possibly a few other locations. He tossed his sporran on the night table.

"Then Louise Cameron, be about your stated agenda, if you please."

She let Liam get his boots off, but then she sat him on the bed, drew his T-shirt over his head, and treated him to the same focused attention Dougie showed his victuals.

"You work out," she said, running her hands over his chest. Her touch was inquisitive and sure, as if he were fresh clay, warm and ready for the wheel and her creative impulses. "But you don't push it with the weights. I like that."

Louise also liked kissing. She'd used her toothbrush while Liam had fed the cat, and she used her imagination as she knelt between Liam's legs and sank her hands into his hair. Her kisses were by turns delicate, plundering, curious, and even shy.

As Liam kissed her back, he waited for the desolation to well, for the sure conviction he was making a fool of himself, for the despair that could rob him of all pleasure.

Louise eased away, arms about his waist, cheek pillowed on his thigh. "I want to savor you, Liam, and I want to throw you on the bed and have at you in case I lose my nerve."

He took the elastic from her hair and set it beside his sporran. "Does that happen? You get this far and wish you'd never asked or accepted?" Did it happen to her *too*?

She nuzzled his parts through the wool of his kilt, an overture as friendly as it was arousing.

"I don't get asked. My brother says I have a No Vacancy light on. You?"

"A widower probably has his own version of the No Vacancy sign. I'm not having second thoughts, Louise. I want to make love with you."

Liam wasn't having second thoughts yet, and didn't sense any lurking. Interesting and a significant relief, or maybe the simple result of accepting overtures from a woman who'd leave in two weeks.

Louise sat up and went to work on the buckles of Liam's kilt. "I didn't know you were a widower, Liam. I'm sorry. Are you all right?" Was he all right? A prosaic, mundane question to which most people expected an equally prosaic reply. Louise unfastened the kilt and flipped the sides open, leaving Liam sitting naked on the bed, Louise kneeling before him.

"I'm doing better. We'll talk."

Because with Louise, Liam could talk. She had a meddling, sometimes insensitive family; she'd made poor career choices; and uncertainty still tried to occasionally steal her breath and her confidence. None of that had followed her up the stairs, and yet it was all a part of who she was and why she appealed to him.

When she stood, Liam pushed her yoga pants off her hips, revealing long legs, interesting knees, and an absence of underwear. Louise picked the yoga pants up with her toes and foot-flung them onto a chair.

"Good aim," Liam remarked, settling his hands on Louise's hips. The artist in him tried to find the right term for the color that was two shades darker than auburn as he coaxed Louise to straddle his lap. While he wrestled with that aesthetic challenge, Louise pulled her T-shirt off and fired it in the direction of the chair too, so they were both naked.

"You don't have to finesse this, Liam. I'm wound up enough—"

He kissed her. "Maybe the problem is, American women don't expect enough of their men, or don't take the time to show the poor blokes how to go on."

And yet, Liam understood Louise's dilemma. She was dealing with a resurgence of desire, a gale-force wind gusting through her mature, rational self-image and her firmly entrenched low expectations. She'd grown accustomed to desire wafting past her life on breezes and zephyrs, not this hurricane of desire and need.

Liam rose with Louise in his arms, her legs twining around his flanks.

"Wall sex?" she asked. "It's fine if you like—"

He tossed her onto the bed. "You tell me, Louise. If you want wall sex, floor sex, doggie sex, oral sex, shower sex, *ceiling* sex—now you're laughing at me, and my charms on display for all to see."

And what a fetching picture she made on the quilt, naked, smiling, and rosy.

"I don't want sex at all. I want Liam Cromarty's lovemaking."

He came down over her on all fours. "Then you shall have it."

The conversation turned tactile, as Louise mapped him with a sure, firm touch. She listened with her hands, stroking down his sides, kneading his bum, tangling her fingers in his hair.

Liam was retaliating with slow, lazy kisses, when Louise turned her head. "Cromarty, you are the most infernally, maddeningly—you're not one of those men who gets turned on by begging, are you? I draw the line—"

Liam eased down onto his forearms and gave her some of his weight. "Louise, you say where and how. I say when. Can we agree on that much?"

"If when is soon."

"Compared to two years, twenty minutes is not—"

"Two *years*, Liam? Oh, honey, I'm so sorry."

Liam kissed her brow. When she called him *honey* in that tone of voice, he was helpless not to kiss some part of her.

"You ought to be pleased not to find yourself on the worktable in the studio," Liam growled, "mud everywhere and a forgotten stylus digging into your tender parts."

"I'd be more pleased if you'd—"

"Spare me from a determined woman." Artists were like this. They fixed on an idea, and had to harp and refine and focus on it until they'd badgered the notion into complete submission.

Liam grabbed his sporran off the night table, found a condom, and put it on. "Are you happy now, Miss Cameron?"

She studied his rampant cock more closely than she had any of the Old Masters at the portrait gallery.

"I'm about to be very happy, Mr. Cromarty."

Liam granted himself a moment to gather his thoughts, to breathe, to take stock, and *be present*. This felt right, felt like moving forward, like trusting in life again.

He positioned himself against Louise, then laced their fingers against the pillow. "Hold on, and tell me if I'm gettin' it wrong."

Louise closed her fingers around his. "Same goes, Cromarty. Hold on, and tell me if I'm getting it wrong."

They got it *right*. Liam joined them slowly, pausing to savor and kiss, and breathe together, to nuzzle and rejoice. Louise matched his rhythm beautifully, untangling one hand to anchor on his bum, her ankles locked at the small of his back. The sheer pleasure of her eagerness, the glory of her sweet heat, the sense of shared desire swamped Liam's entire awareness.

He sent his mind in search of words. "Say when, Louise."

"Liam."

He took that for a *when* and picked up the tempo to slow, hard lunges. Louise clutched at him with gratifying desperation and *when* became *now*, and then, for a moment, *forever*. Pleasure cascaded up through Liam, bringing light, joy, and a sense of well-being so profound he could have wept.

And laughed, and laughed, and laughed.

When he'd stopped heaving like a racehorse, he settled for a smiling kiss to Louise's ear. "God bless America."

She chortled, her belly bouncing against his. "Now look what you've done."

He'd slipped from her body, though the way she patted his backside won her a place in his heart. Gentle, firm, proprietary, protective, and bit scolding.

"No worries," he said, heaving to his hands and knees. "I've another frenchie in my sporran."

She brushed his hair back. "A french—oh. We have other names for them. Only one?"

Lovely woman. "You'll find more in the drawer, but we'll have to replace those. Jeannie would notice."

Louise began carefully unrolling the condom from Liam's softening cock. "At least she doesn't go through the trash."

Morag might. Liam made a mental note to take the trash to his house. "I could have done that, Miss Cameron."

"I'll let you get it the next three times," Louise said. "For now, I need a cuddle."

* * *

Liam's tushy was sufficiently adorable that Louise tried to memorize its contours as he moved from the bed to the bathroom. He left the door open, so she could watch him standing at the sink, washing his hands, then rubbing at himself with a damp washcloth.

He was a man in his prime, gloriously healthy, and an inspiration to anybody with a visual/spatial imagination.

"I want to sketch you," Louise called.

"First you want to cuddle, then you want to sketch," he groused, drying his hands. "Next I suppose you'll be raiding my sporran for a bite of tablet. Fickle is woman."

"You brought me tablet?" Thoughtful of him.

"I usually have some with me, and you seem to enjoy it."

Liam was no boy, and thus he had wounds and scars, parts of himself he kept guarded. Louise would not ask if he always had condoms in that sporran, because he'd already told her—

"Did you check the date on those French whatevers?" she asked as he climbed back into bed.

"I bought them last night," he said. "Had to buy more cat food and grabbed them on the same trip."

Louise wrestled Liam against her side, or pushed and tugged until he figured out where she wanted him.

"You're a friendly sort," Liam remarked, his cheek resting on the slope of her breast. "Though a simple, 'Liam, may I hold you?' might get the job done faster."

Liam, may I fall in love with you? Louise would scare him off if she asked that, and she'd scared herself by even thinking it. They lived on opposite sides of an ocean, for criminy sakes.

She traced the contour of his ear, a more complicated appendage than most people realized—on many levels.

"Liam, may I interrogate you?"

He heaved a seismic male sigh. "I married while I was at uni, her name was Karen. She thought I had ambition, I thought she had a nice laugh. She was an accountant, though she also enjoyed cooking."

Louise waited, because these were the introductory recitations, the ones that not only didn't hurt, they comforted a little.

"We married," Liam said, "and then, I fell in love. With Caravaggio, with Vermeer, with Canaletto, the Venus of Willendorf, the Lascaux cave paintings, Fabergé eggs, and early medieval manuscripts. With all things beautiful and profound and interesting. What my wife thought was ambition was merely passion. I didn't figure that out until it was too late."

Louise stroked her fingers through his hair. "You haven't told this story to anybody, have you?"

"My family knows some of it. That feels good."

So, no. He'd carried these regrets and memories around for years rather than entrust them to another.

"I'll tell you a story when you're through," Louise said. Liam wouldn't laugh at her, wouldn't tell her to stop overreacting and feeling sorry for herself.

He kissed her shoulder. "I'll listen, and there isn't much more to tell of mine. I wrote some articles, comparing porcelain to cave paintings, Vermeer to Warhol. I was too inexperienced and cocky to understand that wasn't the done thing. The galleries loved those articles, the academicians didn't know what to do with them, and in short order, I was Dr. Liam Cromarty, PhD, attending the openings, speaking at the conferences."

"You're not telling me all of it. You got into some pissing contest with another hotshot, you failed to spot a forgery, you stepped in doo-doo somehow."

Liam might be the expert on Vermeer's influence on Fabergé, but Louise had four PhD's in how to step in doo-doo.

"I'm not sure what a pissing contest is," he said, "but suffice it to say, I was so busy racking up frequent-flier miles and being witty and insightful at gallery openings, I lost track of my wife."

"Was she ill?"

Liam wasn't ill, but he was ailing, with regret, with old grief, and with the loneliness those burdens caused. Louise could feel them in him the way she could feel cold at the center of a ball of clay.

"Karen was not ill. She was sick of me, and my silly little academic self-importance. I was growing tired of it myself, tired of being the infallible expert on everything, and the one expected to debunk popular theories and pass judgment on all the new talent."

The bedroom felt cozy rather than gloomy, though the rain was coming down in earnest. Dougie strolled into the room and hopped up on the bed, settling in along Louise's other side.

Good kitty.

"The new talent never ends," Louise said. She'd been new talent once, to the extent the small world of ceramic art had new talent. "And most new talent shouldn't quit the day job no matter how good they are or what the work is selling for."

"I should have stayed home," Liam said, reaching across Louise to pet the cat. "I should have taught my classes and given my wife the children she wanted. When we married, we agreed children were not a priority, and Karen didn't bring it up until I'd finished my doctorate and landed the teaching post. And then…"

The cat's purr added a comforting touch to the gathering.

"Then?" Louise prompted.

"Then she brought up children again. We argued, we made up, we argued again. I wasn't ready, she wasn't getting any younger. We separated off and on for two years. She said the ambition she'd so admired in me had become selfishness and a thousand other faults, and of course, when that's the reception a man gets, he finds reasons to present papers at conferences all over the globe."

The rain gusted, a spatter of droplets rattling against the skylight. Louise fished around in the Magic Man Purse and found the bag of tablet.

"Have one," she said, holding a cube up to Liam's lips. He nibbled obediently. When she kissed him, the flavor lingered, though so did his regret.

"We were separated," he said, softly. "The longest separation so far, and I had made up my mind that if it would make her happy, we'd try for a baby. I loved her, she was my wife, the rest of it—the gallery openings, the keynote speeches, the growing list of publications—they weren't making me happy. They'd made her miserable, and that was no reflection on me or the vows I'd taken."

This would have been easier to hear if Liam had cheated with any woman besides the squat little Venus of Willendorf, if he'd asked for a divorce, if he'd done anything but turn up decent when it really counted.

Louise drew the covers around his shoulders. "Tell me the rest of it."

"We agreed to spend the weekend together at the same cottage where we'd honeymooned. The plan was to talk. I thought I'd come up with the surefire scheme to save the marriage and recover a bit of my self-respect. I'm not sure what Karen had in mind. She listened, she cried, she told me she loved me. Then as we walked around the loch, she collapsed. By the time I'd carried her back to the cottage, she was gone."

"Heart attack? Stroke?" What other sudden death claimed an otherwise healthy young woman?

"Ectopic pregnancy, and before you ask, no. The child could not have been mine."

Well, hell. "This is the bad breakup you mentioned?" The worst breakup imaginable, for what woman conceives another man's child when she's intent on salvaging her marriage?

"Aye. I was so bewildered, and angry and guilty. There's most of a year I can't recall and probably wouldn't want to. I turned mean and condescending, to my colleagues, to my students, to my family. Heavy drinking turned into stupid drinking."

He fell silent for a moment, maybe sorting between bad memories, awful memories, and periods of no memory at all.

"If I'd been a dog," he went on, "somebody would have shot me out of simple kindness, but I was the *brilliant young scholar* who hadn't the sense to do his grieving in private. I had keynote speeches to give on important topics such as romantic elements in post-modern commercial art."

Louise blinked, hard, because tears would not help. They wouldn't help a wife who'd hit the end of her rope. They wouldn't help Liam. They wouldn't help anybody.

"I'm sorry, Liam. I'm so very, very sorry. For you, for her. No wonder you went into a tailspin." Louise pushed him to his back and climbed over him, blanketing him with her body. "Does your family know?"

"Jeannie or Morag might suspect the baby wasn't mine. My younger brothers were certainly concerned. They were all friends with Karen, of a sort. They've never said, and I haven't asked."

Liam was beyond tears, which was sad in itself, but also a relief. Louise would have lost it if he'd been able to cry.

"Who was the father?"

"What does that matter? I failed my wife, left her to loneliness and frustration, and the one thing she asked of me, I denied her. I suspect she was involved with one of the fellows from the art history department, a quiet man who listens well but doesn't publish much."

Louise sat up and brushed Liam's hair away from his brow. His gaze held sadness, but also resignation, and that…that was wrong.

"Liam Cromarty, you are entitled to your grief, to your bad year, to your tailspins and bad days, and regrets. But you've punished yourself long enough, and you'll listen to what I have to say now."

* * *

"Listen to this email," Dunstan Cromarty said to his wife as he joined her on the sofa near the wood stove. "It's from Liam, and he may finally have finished going daft: 'Chauffering your spinster lawyer friend about for the next two weeks as a favor to Jeannie. Miss Cameron likes tablet. Dougie likes her. What do we know about her, other than that she's a Cameron? Love to Jane, Liam.'"

Jane pushed an indignant Wallace off her lap and curled up against her husband.

"If your cousin thinks Louise is a spinster, he's a few drams short of a bottle, Dunstant. At least he e-mailed you."

While Louise had yet to e-mail Jane. Wallace hopped back up and appropriated Dunstan's lap. Atop the piano across the room, Blackstone was busy at his bath.

"I think Liam means the word spinster as a compliment," Dunstan said, scratching the back of Wallace's neck. "Liam is a spinster too."

A mighty handsome one, though Liam was also shy, and married to his job. "How long ago did his wife die?" Jane asked.

"Nearly five years. Liam and Karen were having a rough patch, and he did not cope well. I almost moved home, but my practice was finally starting to take hold. Do you think Louise will come back to the practice of law? She's damned good."

Jane could *feel* Wallace purring, though he did so quietly. She purred when Dunstan petted her too.

"Louise was damned miserable, Dunstan. She's not… Louise has no mean streak, no competitive edge. One of her art professors stole a glazing process she'd developed as an undergrad. She'd been working on it for years, since high school, and he was her adviser. I suspect he was also wooing her, and when he took credit for her work, she just slunk off to law school."

"Don't the senior academic types often take credit for the work their students do?" Dunstan gently unhooked Wallace's front claws from his jeans. "This cat is determined to draw blood."

Wallace had become more territorial since Blackstone had joined the household, though Blackstone was like his owner: very pretty, very self-contained, never imposing, never asking anything of anybody.

"Louise should have raised a stink," Jane said. "Her pottery takes your breath away, and it's simply pottery. This Hellenbore guy was some big deal at the art school, and Louise found out he'd done the same thing five years earlier with another female student's use of mixed media."

Dunstan wrapped an arm across Jane's shoulders. "I don't know what mixed media is, but Louise's cross-examination has taken more than one judge's breath away. You could call her, let her know the family's been fretting over Liam for years."

And make it obvious that Jane was fretting over Louise?

"What then, Dunstan? A half-dozen guys went gaga over Louise in law school, and I think most of the State's Attorney's Office of either gender would love to ask her out. She couldn't be bothered with any of them. Once bitten, twice shy."

"I rather like it when you nibble on me," Dunstan murmured, shifting the cat to the floor. "And I adore nibbling on you."

He demonstrated his adoration on Jane's shoulder, while Jane tried to hold on to her train of thought.

"What if Louise takes a bite out of Liam?" she asked. "Loves him and leaves him? She could do that—no chance of things getting messy if you're packing a round-trip ticket."

Which Jane had insisted on—like an idiot. .

The cat hopped up again and marched across Jane to resume his place on Dunstan's lap.

"Jane, my dearest love, I'm every bit as worried Liam will avail himself of Louise's charms and then wave her on his way. Jeannie says for a year or so, he occasionally dallied, but never gave his heart away, and then he stopped even dallying. This e-mail is not from a man smitten by true love."

"They're adults," Jane said, scratching the cat's chin, which provoked more soft rumbling. "They'll sort it out."

Dunstan was quiet for a moment. He wasn't a loud husband. He was a hardworking and calm husband—also cunning.

"What are you thinking, Dunstan Cromarty?"

"I'll tell Liam if he hurts Louise, you'll kill him."

Well, that was honest. "And if Louise hurts him?"

"You'll have to kill her, my dear. I'll be too busy worrying about my cousin."

* * *

Louise Cameron in a stern mood—when naked—was an imposing, alluring sight. Liam's mind filled with images of Nike, goddess of victory, fierce and lovely, both.

"I'm listening, Louise."

"Karen could have fought for you."

Liam resisted the urge to get his mouth on Louise's nipples, which were one shade darker than her lips. That color, a delicate, rococo blend of pink, cream, and—old gold, maybe?—would forever after be *"Louise"* to him.

And the daft woman wanted to lecture him. "Karen and I fought. I didn't enjoy it."

"She probably didn't either, but I'm saying she could have fought *for* you."

"Come here," Liam said, urging Louise down to his chest. "I'm a visual thinker, you see, and my concentration isn't up to the strain presented by your many charms."

He'd made her laugh, which led him to hope she'd leave off nattering about Kar—

"She was your wife, Liam. Did she ever read the papers you wrote?"

Liam traced his way, bump by bump, down Louise's spine. "She wasn't an art historian." As a young husband, he'd been baffled by what seemed to him an indifference to beauty. Karen hadn't been indifferent to beauty. She'd been indifferent to Liam's passion for it.

"Anybody should be able to grasp the substance of whatever you wrote for the galleries or general readership magazines."

"I suppose." Liam had written enough of those articles. Pointless, all of them.

"Did Karen ever join you for a conference?"

"What would she have done at a portraiture conference, or a conference on Dutch Renaissance masters?"

"Liam, if I took you to Amsterdam for a long weekend at a legal conference, you'd find a way to entertain yourself. Same with New York, San Francisco, Rome. Even an accountant has leave, and you had frequent-flier miles."

Liam's sense of well-being ebbed, leaving his old friends weariness and bewilderment in its place. Louise made the same arguments Liam had made— for the last two interminable years of his marriage.

Come with me, please. To the opening, to the conference, to the reception.

"She could have gone to counseling with you," Louise went on. "She could have suggested a second honeymoon, audited one of your courses. She could have waited. She could have done foster care for older children. When people come to me for a divorce, they've often been struggling for ten years, in and out of counseling, changing jobs so they commute less or make more, trying a different neighborhood, or taking ballroom dance classes. They try *anything*, and they fight for their marriages. Karen whined for a couple years about a baby when she knew children weren't a priority for you."

Liam wanted to stuff his head under the pillow, except a small, exhausted, battle-weary part of him refused to hide from Louise's logic.

We shouldn't speak ill of the dead.
Karen's not here to defend herself.
I neglected my wife.
I should have tried harder.

The accusations of his conscience, all served up with a dram or three of whisky, which was perhaps the local equivalent of serving pecan pie to a girl struggling with her weight.

Liam wasn't angry at Karen for dying. He was angry at her for taking a piece of his soul with her—*and he had been angry long enough.*

"You are so fierce, Louise Cameron," he said, cradling her jaw between his hands. "Enough talk, enough dwelling on the past. We're alive, and there's no place I'd rather be, nobody I'd rather be with, nothing I'd rather be doing. Make love with me."

The words were a spell, an incantation, that brought a quiet *joie de vivre* trickling back through him.

And they were the truth. Liam leaned up and kissed Louise, not politely or tenderly, but like a man starved for her ferocity and ready to shower his own upon her.

The cat leaped off the bed, Louise laughed, and then she kissed the hell out of Liam while she fished on the night table for his sporran.

CHAPTER FIVE

Louise saved Culloden Battlefield for a sunny, mild day. The site of a battle that had cost a nation its hopes of holding the British throne, and much, much more, was sobering even in spring sunshine. Liam was quiet as they walked the paths over the moor.

"This place is lovely," Louise said, "and that feels… both wrong and right."

"Wrong that they should have died amid such beauty, right that they should rest here," Liam said. "Shall we sit?"

Any Scot would be sobered by a visit to Culloden, where Scot had fought against Scot by the thousands, and post-battle retaliation by the Crown had been so harsh as to become a foundational component of the national psyche.

"Is there a silver lining?" Louise asked, taking Liam's hand. "The land is still a boggy moor, but did any good come of this?"

Had the American Civil War produced any silver linings? Did any war?

"The clans haven't massacred each other since," Liam said. "But then, after Culloden, the clans were all but obliterated in a political sense. May I change the subject?"

An older couple strolled by, hand in hand, accompanied by a terrier in a Royal Stewart plaid jacket who sniffed the grass beside the path, then trotted ahead.

"Of course you can change the subject," Louise said, because her time in Scotland had dwindled to days, and they'd yet to talk about what came next.

If anything. Twice Louise had been ready to have that conversation, and twice Liam's phone had rung at the exact wrong moment. He'd taken the calls, business of some sort, and Louise had wandered off to nibble tablet or admire the infinite shades of green that were Scotland in spring.

Liam kissed her knuckles, one of the countless small gestures of affection with which he was so generous.

"What I'd like to ask you is this: You told me last week that Karen could have fought for me rather than with me," he said. "Is there somebody who should have fought for you?"

A man who saw aesthetic parallels between stone fertility figures and Georgian portraiture would make that leap, and abruptly, the bleak battlefield was the perfect location for what needed to be said.

"Yes, Liam. Somebody should have fought for me, and instead threw down their weapons without firing a shot. When I was finishing up at art school, the champion who failed to join battle was *me*. I knuckled under, to Aunt Ev, to pecan pie, to common sense."

Fighting had never occurred to Louise, not against her family, not against Hellenbore, not against her own broken heart.

"I'm sorry," Liam said. "When we're young, we're reckless about wading into a fight, but often for the wrong causes. Is there a way to make it right?"

Interesting question. The terrier went yapping off into the treacherous, swampy ground that had been the end of so many hopes nearly three hundred years ago. When the old man whistled, the dog came loping back to him.

"How do you make something like that right?" Louise murmured, letting her head rest on Liam's shoulder. "I was lied to, my work misrepresented, and my future knocked on its ass. I knew I had talent, and yet all I did was go home to my parents, and apply to law school."

"You're making it right every time you sit at your wheel," Liam said. "Atonement can take time."

He spoke from experience, and his tale wanted telling, so Louise held back the details of her own regrets.

"Before Karen died—I can say those words now, and they only ache, they don't decimate—before Karen died, when I was racketing about, holding forth on three continents about some damned sculpture or kylix, I was befriended by several of the New York critics."

That bunch. Most critics lacked the gift of creation, so many of them turned to destruction instead. Boggy ground, indeed.

"This doesn't end well," Louise said. If she and Liam had been in bed—Liam slept at the cottage now—she would have climbed on top of him and held on tight.

"It ends," he said, his arm coming around Louise's shoulders. "Sometimes, that's the best we can do. One older fellow chatted me up at every opportunity, always bringing up the latest collections, the latest first shows, the latest articles. I never suspected he was using my half-pickled insights, my off-the-cuff opinions, to recycle into his blog posts. He was clever with words, but his grasp of art sadly wanting, and he was unkind."

Someone had figuratively stolen Liam's glazes. Amazing, how angry Louise was on his behalf, while for herself she'd been simply hurt and ashamed.

Amazing too, the comfort she took from Liam's hand in hers, and his arm around her shoulders.

"You put the bullets into the gun he fired at others' hopes and creativity, Liam, but he fired the gun, not you."

"If I'd had any aspirations toward art criticism, that experience put me off them permanently. Some of the damage he did others haunted me for years, though I took what steps I could to make things right. The advantage he took of my carelessness helped me put aside the hard liquor."

The old couple had walked around nearly the entire battlefield now, their pace measured, though they moved as one unit.

"I want to capture this," Louise said. "I want that couple, their enduring connection, and the way it blesses even this place. I want a wheel where I can throw the love and the sorrow, both, and finish it with a hundred colors nobody has seen before. I'm not going back into that law office, Liam. I know that now."

He kissed her cheek, on that bleak, sunny bench, and Liam Cromarty could say volumes with his kisses. *I'm proud of you. I'm glad for you. You'll do it. Your dreams are worthy. You deserve to be happy.*

But was he saying *I love you?*

Louise loved Liam. Loved how with him she could talk about anything or simply be silent with him.

"You never finished your own story, Louise," he said, tugging her to her feet. "The one about art school, and not standing up for yourself. If you thought law school was a place to lick your wounds, then you were at a sorry pass."

They wandered along in the same direction as the older couple, who'd apparently made their circuit and gone back into the battlefield museum.

"I didn't need to *feel* in law school, Liam. I only needed to think, get enough sleep, and get the assignments done. With my senior art school project, I fell afoul of one or those critics. My adviser claimed any critical notice was good for aspiring artists, so when the great and powerful Stephen Saxe brought his minions on a tour of the campus gallery, the entire senior class was nearly drunk with anxiety."

In the middle of the battlefield, Liam stopped and put his arms around Louise. He said nothing, so she fortified herself with his affection.

"Saxe went after my showing," she said, "tore it to shreds, said it was well executed but at best a slavish tribute to the new glazing technique my adviser had debuted the previous weekend at his show downtown. If after four years of study at the knee of a master, all I could do was derivative work, then maybe my degree should be in Teacher's Pet, not art."

Louise waited for Liam to say something, to console, to philosophize, to heap scorn on the head of the critic who'd be so cruel to a mere student, or the professor who'd steal credit for her creative accomplishment.

"I knew Saxe," Liam said, eventually. "I learned to avoid him. I'm so very sorry, Louise." For a progression of moments, bathed in sunshine and spring breezes, he simply held her while she gathered her courage.

"Hellenbore stole my process," she said, the first time she'd spoken those words out loud to somebody who might grasp their full import. "He set up his own show, and I'm nearly certain he arranged for Saxe to make that royal progress to a mere student exhibition for the express purpose of wrecking my career before I had a career. I never saw it coming, but that experience taught me to anticipate the ambushes even in the courtroom, and never threaten with a figuratively empty gun."

Liam knew the art world, was part of it, and should have been one person to whom Louise could confide this story and earn some commiseration.

He dropped his arms, took her hand, and resumed walking. "Guns are dangerous to all in their ambit, Louise. I can see why you'd not enjoy the legal profession."

The comment was… off. Not the Liam she knew and wanted desperately to love. Scotland's outlook on guns wasn't the same as what Louise had grown up with, but Liam wasn't talking about firearms.

"I never figured out how to bring suit against Hellenbore," Louise said, "or how to get even with Saxe, but I became good at being a lawyer, up to a point. The law is the law and the rules are the rules, but the rules can go only so far toward solving the problems we create with each other. That drove me crazy."

"Maybe it drove you un-crazy," Liam said, passing her a piece of tablet. "You've found your art again, or you soon will."

Louise took a bite and gave Liam back the rest. Next would come the shared bottle of water, or perhaps they'd stop in the museum's snack shop for soup, bread, and butter.

A few days in a borrowed studio wasn't finding her art again, though those days had been lovely.

"Did you stop eating meat when Karen died?"

"Aye."

"Because she was a good cook, and the kitchen smells reminded you of her?"

"You're very astute. I didn't figure it out so quickly, but by then I was out of the carnivore habit. Shall I take a picture of you?"

This place had put Liam's mood off. He was present and he was dodging into shadows, much like the man who'd met her at the airport.

"I want a picture of us, Liam."

"I'm not very photogenic, how about if I—" He got his phone out of his sporran. "I'll take you and you take me?"

He was the most photogenic man Louise had ever met, and this prevarication wasn't like him.

"Not good enough, Cromarty. I know Culloden is a sad place, but I'm happy to be here with you." Louise flagged down a couple chattering in German and gestured and smiled them into taking a photo of her and Liam against the stone cairn at the center of the battle field.

The image was well composed and well exposed, though Liam's smile was pained, his eyes bleak.

"Shall I send you a copy?" Louise asked.

Liam peered at the screen of her phone, coming close enough to put a hint of woodland and heather on the morning breeze.

"We'll do better elsewhere, I think. Are you thirsty?"

"Sure." Louise swilled from the bottle of Highland Spring, then passed it to Liam when she wanted to throw her arms around him.

Even to tell him she loved him, though this sad morning on a battlefield wasn't the time or place.

"C'mon," she said, taking his hand. "Let's blow this popsicle stand and head down to Cairngorms National Park. They have reindeer there, don't they? We don't have reindeer in Georgia, and if we did, we'd probably hunt them to extinction."

* * *

Liam had bought a damned ring yesterday, while Louise had been engrossed in her wheel. An emerald stone, more valuable than diamonds and appropriate for Louise's fire and sense of purpose. The setting was Celtic gold, and the sentiments...

Louise had put the heart back in him, and Liam didn't want her to leave, ever.

Though now, the sooner he put her on that plane, the better for them both.

As Louise boiled up a batch of gnocchi, Liam opened the wine and prepared to lie his way through the rest of Louise's visit.

"Will you throw tonight?" he asked. Louise could work at her wheel for hours, and he had the sense she was only warming up. Five years' penance for another's crimes rode her hard, and she'd throw her way free of it.

"Nah. No throwing tonight. Tromping around all day wore me out. If you'll slice the bread, I'll set the table."

At every meal Liam ate with his family, every single meal, somebody had to make a joke about his decision to stop eating meat. Louise hadn't remarked on it once. When they planned meals, her suggestions were meatless, and she was the next thing to a cheese connoisseur.

They'd toured a distillery in Inverness, and she'd made the most awful face at one of the world's best-loved Highland single malts.

Of course, Liam had bought her a ring, and fool that he was, returning it would about kill him. He'd been about killed before and didn't care to repeat the experience.

"Shall I dress the salad?" Louise asked.

"Please, and I'll pour."

Louise chose the wines, because Louise chose the cheeses. Main dishes were Liam's province, and salads and dessert were negotiated.

Though what in God's name would they talk about now?

Say, Louise, did you know that Saxe's insults to your work weren't even original? I sneered and snickered my way past all those lovely vases, those intriguing drinking cups, and the teapot that shed rainbows in all directions, though even I admitted a student's derivative work was superior to what Hellenbore had displayed a week earlier.

Saxe had left that part out, of course. Liam took a sip of wine, but just a sip. He'd earned this misery, and by God, he'd endure it.

Though not alone. Before conversation could turn awkward or intimate, Uncle Donald came clomping onto the porch.

"I smell dinner," he said, setting his tackle down outside the front door. "Don't suppose there's room for a lonely old man at the table?"

"A shameless man in his prime," Louise said, joining Liam at the door. "The boots can stay out here, though, and you will wash your hands."

"I like her," Donald said, toeing off a pair of green Wellies. "Has a confident air and a nice behind."

"No dessert for you, auld man," Louise said over her shoulder. "We're politically correct at Dunroamin Cottage, if we know what's good for us."

For once, Liam was affirmatively glad to see his uncle, who could tell story after story, about everything from the Battle of the Shirts to Mary Queen of Scots, to epic rounds of golf at St. Andrews.

When the meal had been consumed, the coffee and tablet had made the rounds, and Donald had told stories on half the Cromarty clan, he kissed Louise's cheek and rose.

"I'll be off then. Shall I feed your puppy, Liam?"

"You have *a puppy*?" Louise asked.

"He has an old blind dog," Donald said. "Or half-blind. She's good company fishing, is Helen."

"Helen's getting on," Liam said, taking his dishes to the sink. "She's not blind in the least, but she is good company if you're inclined to stay in one spot for hours."

"If you like spending time with bears," Donald said, snitching another piece of tablet. "Louise strikes me as the better bargain."

Louise rose and shoved the mostly empty wine bottle at him. "Time to go, you. Comparing ladies to dogs is no way to win friends and influence women. Don't forget your fishing pole."

Liam loved hearing Louise talk. Bits of Georgia crept in—fishin' pole, instead of fishing rod, or rod and reel—and her tone was always warm.

"I'll do the dishes if you want to take your shower," he said when Donald had gone stomping on his way, singing about the rashes-o, and drinking from the bottle.

I don't want to be like that. Liam didn't want to be old and alone, smelling of river mud, swilling leftover wine, and deriving a sense of usefulness by feeding a dog who barely woke up between meals anymore.

"I'm dead on my feet," Louise said, putting plastic wrap over the salad. "If you're sure you don't mind cleaning up, I'll see you upstairs."

Reprieve. Another forty-five minutes when Liam wouldn't have to make conversation, wrestle guilt, and count the minutes until Louise's departure. He kissed her cheek and patted her bottom.

"Away with you, then, madam. Dougie and I will manage. Don't wait up for us."

She hugged him—Louise was unstinting with her affection, something Liam would not have guessed about her when he'd fetched her from the airport.

And then she was gone, leaving Liam with a messy kitchen, and more heartache than one tired, lonely Scot should have to bear.

* * *

By Louise's last day at the cottage, an invisible elephant in pink Scottish plaid had joined her vacation entourage. The elephant carried around a load of questions nobody was asking anybody.

So, what happens after the plane takes off?

Will you call me?

Will I see you again?

Liam made endlessly tender, quiet love to her, then came at her with ferocious passion. Then it was Louise's turn to be tender, to memorize the turn of his shoulders, the line of his flanks, the texture of his skin at the small of his back.

She spent hours at the wheel and more hours online doing research—about glazes, collections, art schools, and the past. Hellenbore had retired amid some scandal involving an undergraduate "prone to depression."

"She should be furious, not depressed," Louise informed the drinking cup on the wheel. "But if she forced him into retirement, maybe she should be proud."

The cup spun on the wheel, perfectly symmetric, but plain. No colors, no variations in texture or form to give it life.

"You need to eat," Liam said from the doorway. He watched her from time to time, but he neither answered questions nor asked them lately. The studio hardly had room for Louise's heartache, Liam's quiet presence, and that damned pink elephant.

"I need to finish up," Louise said, dragging the cutoff wire under her clay. "I'll be an hour at least cleaning the knives, scrapers, and other tools. You don't have to help."

Liam's brows twitched. As an older man, he'd have bushy brows. That single twitch confirmed that Louise's elephant was getting restless, putting a sharpness on her words she hadn't intended.

By this time tomorrow, Louise would have left Scotland, possibly forever.

"I can make dinner," Liam said. "I notice you haven't started to pack."

Whatever the hell that meant.

Louise mashed the clay back into a hard, compact ball. "I'm quick when it comes to throwing my things into a suitcase. If we're making pizza, we'll need ingredients. I'll clean up, you make a grocery run, and we'll meet in the kitchen."

"Sounds like a plan."

Liam sauntered over to her, kissed the top of her head, and would have left, except Louise caught his clean hand in her muddy one.

"I'll miss you, Liam. I'll miss you terribly."

Another kiss. "Likewise, Louise Mavis Cameron."

Then he was gone.

Louise dealt with the tools of her trade—her art—and tidied up the studio until it was as clean and welcoming as she'd found it. She grabbed a shower for good measure and was toweling off when another question joined her already overflowing supply.

How had Liam known her middle name? She'd never told him, not specifically, which middle name went with which Cameron sister, and yet he'd known her middle name was Mavis.

Interesting.

* * *

Words stuck in Liam's throat all the way to the airport, while beside him, Louise held her peace. A woman who'd been cheated out of her future as an artist by a lot of stupid, arrogant men probably learned to keep her own counsel very well.

"Are you nervous?" Liam asked as they tooled over the Forth Road Bridge.

"I have it on good authority that flying to the States is easier than flying to Europe. What will you do with yourself today, Liam?"

He'd get the cottage ready for Jeannie's next rental, respond to the emails he'd neglected for the past two weeks, and get on with the business of hating himself for the rest of his life—again.

"I'll catch up on the housework, mostly."

They reached the southern bank of the firth, that much closer to the airport.

"Liam, you have a beautiful house. I didn't poke around inside, though when I took Helen back yesterday, I couldn't help but admire it. Somebody went to a lot of trouble with that house, a lot of expensive trouble."

This was a question he could answer. "How do I afford that place on a college professor's salary?"

"You have art everywhere. Nice art."

"That's not only art, that's inventory, Louise. For years, when I saw something I liked, I bought it. Small things at first, then larger pieces. You'd be surprised what major corporations and even law firms are willing to pay for a bit of the pretty for their offices."

Louise left off pretending to be fascinated with the traffic around them. "You're a *dealer*? That's why you get phone calls from all over the world and jabber away in French and German?"

"Not quite a dealer," Liam said. "I don't sell the pieces I own, I rent them out. When a client wants a different look, I find them something else, from what's on hand, in storage, or in various galleries that know what I like. It's rather profitable."

The smile Louise aimed at him was both admiring and knowing. "That's why you don't bring it up with your family? You're embarrassed to make money at something you enjoy?"

Liam would miss Louise for the rest of his life, miss her quickness, her understanding, her passion for cheese, and the way she held entire conversations with a lump of wet clay.

"I simply don't know how to tell them," Liam said. "I make money, the world has a little more good art to enjoy, the businesses are happy, the artists have a paying client and the occasional commission. It doesn't seem fair that I'd also enjoy the work."

The airport was only a few minutes ahead, and yet, what more could Liam say?

I ruined your career years ago, but don't mind that, because sometime in the past two weeks, I fell in love with you.

"You'll let Jeannie know when you're home?" he asked.

"Sure. Or I can text you."

"Please do. I'll worry." And probably kick hard objects, yell at the cat, and ignore messages from family. Familiar territory.

After more pained silence, Liam drew up to the departures curb. "I can park if you like."

"No need," Louise said, opening her door. "I've got this, Cromarty, and I want you to know something."

Liam wrestled Louise's colorful suitcase onto the curb and prepared to die right there in the Scottish spring sunshine that had so captivated her two weeks ago.

"I'll miss you, Louise Cameron. I'll miss you sorely."

"I'll miss you, too. Terribly, horribly, awfully, very badly, but here's something to think about, Professor. I spent some time online last night. If I wanted to earn a master of fine arts, some of the best programs in the world are in your backyard. Some of the most interesting and respected programs, right down the lane in Glasgow."

What is she saying?

Louise wrapped Liam in a fierce embrace.

"You'd come back here, to Scotland, Louise?"

"I can throw pots wherever there's a wheel and mud. I can hand-build. I can sketch. I can teach. I can wait tables, muck stalls, or impersonate a lawyer. What I cannot do anymore, ever again, is let my life go by while I wait for happiness to find me. You're right: I need to do what makes me happy, even if I have to fight for it."

Louise kissed his cheek, then stepped back and grabbed the handle of her suitcase. "Thank you, Liam Cromarty. For everything, thank you."

Liam stood staring long after Louise had disappeared into the crowd, until the blare of an insistent horn reminded him that he was holding up traffic. He didn't recall driving back to Perthshire, but he was still pondering Louise's words when he got home and found Uncle Donald dozing in a chair on his front terrace.

"You're an idiot," Donald said, not even opening his eyes.

Liam took a place beside him, sitting right on the hard stones of the terrace. "Aye, and you're where I get it from."

"Lad, you cannot let that one go. Move to America, commute across the ocean, or kidnap her, but don't waste any more time wallowing in your guilt and grief. You'll end up singing to the fish and wondering how seventy-five years can pass in a summer."

Dougie joined the discussion, hopping onto Donald's lap.

"Donald, I've wronged that woman, and I didn't admit it to her. Isn't it better that she recall me as a Highland fling than learn that I played a significant part in her worst betrayals?"

No, it was not. Having put Louise on the plane, Liam hated the thought of letting his lies and silence be the last chapter in their story. Could he make it right?

Could he ever make it right?

Helen came panting around the side of the house, wet from the shoulders down and reeking of the river. She shook—of course—baptizing Liam and annoying Dougie too.

"You were a right mess for a bit," Donald said, not uncharitably. "Graduate school and all that whatnot with Karen. That's behind you now. A cat, a smelly dog, and a tipsy old man aren't very good company compared to the lass."

They were good company. Louise was better company.

"Louise makes the most beautiful ceramics you've ever seen, Donald. You did see some of it when I first moved into the house. The perfect blend of shapes, colors, textures... She has magic in her heart."

She still had the magic, maybe more than ever. Liam had felt it vibrating through her when she'd been at her wheel, had gloried in its reflection when they'd made love.

"*Louise* made all those vases and pots and dishes? The blue and the green, and peacocky stuff?"

"When she was only a student. I've rented most of her pieces to a New York law firm that won't send them back to me willingly. That firm represents obscenely successful artists, and her work is exactly what they wanted to grace their common areas. I hadn't connected L. Mavis Cameron with my Louise Cameron."

"Well, then," Donald said, passing Liam the cat and rising. "You have matters to see to, Liam. You'd best get on with them."

Dougie bopped Liam's chin, seconding the motion, apparently.

"Classes start back up in a week, Donald, and Louise wasn't exactly reluctant to get on that plane." Because she was off in search of happiness, and what woman wouldn't relish such a quest?

Donald stopped halfway across the terrace to pet Helen's shaggy head. "Sooner begun is sooner done, Liam Donald Cromarty. That woman made you happy, and I'd about given up on you."

Liam had about given up on himself. "You think I should fight for her." So did Liam.

"You're not the brightest of my nephews, but you usually come to the right answer eventually. Am I wrong, Liam?"

Liam rose, the cat in his arms. For two weeks, he'd had somebody to share his meals with, also his bed, and his heart. Those two weeks had been the best he could recall.

"I'm saying you're right, Uncle, but this is a battle I must win, and putting together my strategy will take some time."

"I'll be at the river," Donald said, disappearing down the steps. "If you should take a notion to travel, I'll look in on your beasts."

"You heard him," Liam informed the dog and cat. "I'd best get busy. In New York the day's already half over."

* * *

Liam didn't call, he didn't e-mail. He'd replied to the text Louise had sent two weeks ago confirming her safe return to the United States.

"Rejoicing in your safe arrival there, missing you here. Will be in touch. Throw splendid pots until then. Liam Cromarty."

Not, "Love, Liam."

Not, "Yours, Liam."

Not fondly, sincerely, truly yours…

Louise smashed her clay flat again.

"Are you angry at that clay?" Jane set down the carry out Eritrean on the studio's work table. The space was rented, the light entirely artificial, and the wheel grouchy.

"I did better work in Scotland," Louise said. "I can't focus here. What is wrong with me that I'm attracted to men who—"

Louise's phone rang, blaring "Scotland the Brave," about which Jane apparently knew better than to comment.

"My hands are muddy," Louise said. "Would you get that?"

Though in Scotland, it would be barely seven a.m. Would Liam call that early?

"I'm not getting this," Jane said. "You're letting it ring through. It's Robert."

"And I had no appetite before the phone rang." Robert and his latest scholarly piece of tripe could abuse semicolons on somebody else's watch. Let his Sweet Young Thing help him get published. "I have pots to throw."

"Wash your hands," Jane said, arranging carry-out containers on the work table. "I brought you a heather ale to try. Dunstan likes it for a change of pace."

Louise turned on the tap at the sink and scrubbed at her hands. Did Liam enjoy heather ale? Was he back at his classes? Had he gone fishing with Donald lest his uncle get too lonely?

"Earth to Louise."

"How is Dunstan?" Louise asked, shutting off the tap and taking a whiff of vegetable sambusas Liam would have delighted in. She should have made them for him, with a nice peppery—

"Dunstan is worried about his cousin Liam." Jane said.

Louise slammed the lid of the container shut. If she'd had clay in her hands, she would have thrown it against the wall.

"Do not mess with me, Jane DeLuca Cromarty. I'm PMSing and nursing a broken heart, my muse is playing hard to get, and I'm about to give notice that I won't be teaching in the fall. Is Liam okay?"

Jane set down her unopened bottle of ale, slowly. "You already quit the lawyer day job, Louise. Are you quitting the artist day job, too?"

"Is. Liam. All. Right?"

"Dunstan can't tell. Liam's preoccupied, according to the family grapevine, but not like he was after his wife died. They're not sure what's up, but Uncle Donald's keeping a close eye on him."

"Uncle Donald isn't exactly a good influence." But he was a cagey old guy who knew a thing or two about loneliness. Louise opened her ale and passed Jane the bottle opener. "I'm tempted to delete Robert's message."

Louise took a sip of fermented grain and Scotland.

"You deleted Robert from your bedroom that's a start," Jane said around a mouthful of spongy, vinegary injera bread.

Did Liam even like Eritrean cuisine?

"Robert was never there much to begin with," Louise said. "For the last six months, nobody was asking and nobody was telling. He claimed he was on writing deadlines. Leave me some bread."

Jane divided the remaining bread in half. "Robert's in New York. If you move up there for the privilege of reminding him to put the seat down until he finds some other female to sponge off of, I will smack you."

Liam had made sure Louise was never at risk for that kind of behavior again.

"I like this ale," Louise said, peering at the label. "Fraoch is the Gaelic word for heather."

"And Liam is the Gaelic word for heartache," Jane retorted. "Dunstan says Liam has left town, and Donald isn't saying where he went."

Maybe to a cottage near a loch in the Highlands, maybe to purchase more art.

"He's not headed here that I know of," Louise said. "He said he'd be in touch, but that might be Scottish for 'don't let the door hit ya where the good Lord split ya.'"

"You can take the woman out of Georgia…" Jane said. "You going back to Scotland?"

The damned phone rang again. "Robert," Louise said, putting the phone in silent mode. "He must have already run off his Sweet Young Thing."

Jane tore off another strip of bread. "Revenge is mine, sayeth the former girlfriend, but you honestly couldn't be bothered, could you?"

"With Robert? I knew better, Jane. Before law school, when Hellenbore took such an interest in my glazes and was so encouraging, I was an innocent. Robert was… a distraction."

A lousy distraction.

Jane closed one eye and peered down inside her bottle of ale, managing to look both elegant and silly.

"So if Liam called you in the next fifteen minutes and asked you to join him for a Roman holiday, you'd tell him he's had his shot, one and done?"

"If Liam called, we'd talk about where we go from here," Louise said, assuming her little heart didn't go pitty-patting away with her brain at the sight of even his phone number. "I'd take time to think about any decisions, and he'd understand why."

If Liam could fly to Rome, he could fly to DC. If he could call Singapore, he could call Louise.

"You're not eating much, Louise."

Dunstan would inhale any leftovers Jane took back to the office. Louise used the bread to scoop up another mouthful of spicy potatoes.

"I miss him, Jane. I really, really miss him. He's dear, lovely, an adult, hot, thoughtful…."

"And not calling you," Jane said. "Give it time. Dunstan sometimes takes a while to figure things out. We sort through legal cases together in nothing flat, but family stuff always takes longer."

"You're a good friend."

The phone buzzed, knocking against the table.

"Answer the idiot," Jane said, taking a sip of ale.

Louise glanced at the phone, intending to let Robert's pestering go to voice mail for the third time.

Her stomach gave a funny little hop at the digits crowding her screen. "It's Liam."

CHAPTER SIX

Jane saluted Louise with her bottle of ale. "Give cousin Liam my love, and then read his beads for not calling. Sooner."

"This is Louise." Steady voice, always a good way to start off.

"Liam here."

Two beautiful, Scottish words, and not quite steady. Was that good? "How are you, Liam?" *Where are you? When can I see you again?*

"Exhausted, but I thought I owed you a bit of warning in case you're entertaining."

"Warning about what? And I am entertaining."

A pause, and not because the call was international. "Shall I call back, Louise?"

She glanced at the wall clock. "Give me fifteen minutes, Liam, and Jane says hello."

"Jane? Dunstan's Jane?" The relief in his voice was sweet.

"The very one. We're having lunch, and she sends her love. When I've run her off and charged up my battery for a few minutes, you can call me back."

"I'll do that. Talk soon."

Louise put the phone back on ring and stared at it. "He called, but."

"But nothing. He called. If you're not going to eat that bread, I will or Dunstan will. I'm off, and I *will* expect a report by close of business, Louise. Liam is family, and Dunstan's worried about him."

In other words, Jane was worried about Louise.

Louise tore off a nibble of bread. "Liam sounded fine, but... focused. He has an agenda." He'd always had an itinerary for their day. She suspected he'd taken an itinerary to bed with them, too, and they always reached their destination.

Several times.

Jane packed up her half of the largely uneaten meal. "When a man calls with an agenda, then his objective is not ditching you, though I can understand why you might want to ditch him."

"Go," Louise said. "I want to listen to what Liam has to say, and not only because his accent is luscious."

Jane left with a hug and a kiss, bustling off to make Damson County dangerous for opposing counsel, and doubtless to make a report to Dunstan.

"If I moved to Scotland," Louise told her silent wheel, "Jane would visit, because Dunstan's folks are there."

Scotland had cast a spell independent of Liam. The light; the sense of an orderly society balanced with a long, tumultuous history; the natural beauty... the tablet.

"Aunt Ev would *not* visit, a definite plus."

The studio had a single comfortable chair, over by the one north-facing window. Louise took her ale there, cracked the window, and sat down to wait for the longest nine minutes since minutes had been invented.

* * *

Liam had had such hopes for his plan when he'd been in Scotland, but now... He should have called, he should have discussed this with Louise, he should have waited.

He could not wait. He dialed, heart thumping against his ribs.

"Hello, Liam."

"Has Jane left?" The soul of charm, he would never be. "I mean, how are you, Louise?"

He'd meant: I've missed you, every night, every day, everywhere.

"Jane executed a tactical, if dignified, retreat. I never asked you: Do you like Eritrean food?"

Would an upset woman ask such a thing? Would an *indifferent* woman ask that question?

"I enjoy the vegetarian dishes and particularly the bread. It wants a good ale, though."

"I like you, Liam. I do not like waiting two weeks for you to *be in touch*."

They'd been a busy, fraught two weeks. "In future, I'll call more frequently." He wouldn't overtly promise that. Louise had probably heard plenty of sly, casual promises from men. "I would enjoy the occasional call from you as well, Louise, in case you were wondering."

"I'm wondering," Louise said, the hint of a Southern accent adding nuances to a mere two words.

"About?"

"Aboot? I've missed hearing your voice, Liam. I've wondered how you are, how the classes for the new term are shaping up, and if you're happy."

A hint of reproach with an entire hug's worth of caring. Liam cast around for something witty, sophisticated, and charming to offer in return.

And failed. "I miss everything about you." Pray God the condition was temporary. "Will you meet me in New York this weekend?"

An indrawn breath and then a pause. "New York is not my favorite place."

Well, of course not. Louise had attended art school there, and nobody wanted to revisit the scene of their worst nightmares.

"I have a meeting to attend Friday in the city," Liam said. "We can stay out in Connecticut, the Hudson Valley, wherever you please. I'd really like to see you."

Fight for us, Louise. Please, I'm begging you, fight for us. Though if she declined, Liam would simply drive down to Maryland and put his case before her there. New York was important to his plans, but Louise was indispensable to his happiness.

"Cromarty, your technique needs work. You, I want to see. New York, I don't much care for. Next time we do this, it won't be New York."

Relief, sweet and precious, coursed through him. "Next time we do this, we'll follow your itinerary to the letter. Come up Friday afternoon, and we'll go out for dinner. I want to take you somewhere fancy."

"Do you like heather ale?"

"When a Scotsman says he wants to spend a fortune on your meal, you ask about ale?"

"You've never been parsimonious, Professor. Not in any sense. Find us a hotel in the Village, and I'll take the train up from Baltimore. I'll text you the details."

Liam didn't want to break the connection. "Or you could call me, anytime."

"I just might, but for now, I have pots to throw, Liam. Stay out of trouble until I can get my hands on you."

And mine on you. "I'll do that. See you Friday, Louise, and thank you."

* * *

For Louise, the thrown pot was the canvas, and the finish work—the glazing and texturing, the etched designs, the surface ornamentation—was where she expressed the greater part of her creativity. Shape, contour, heft, and other physical properties of ceramic art all mattered, but appearance made the first and greatest impact for her.

After Liam's call, Louise allowed herself to glaze, fire, and finish a piece for the first time in five years. She was rooting in her shoulder bag for that small vase when she decided to instead grab her cell phone and check e-mail.

She still hadn't dealt with messages Robert had left several days ago.

The train was barreling toward Penn Station, where Liam would meet her, and Louise wasn't about to listen to Robert's messages once she and Liam had connected.

The last two messages were simply, "C'mon Louise, call me," and "This is rude behavior between colleagues, Lou. Pick up, would you?'"

Colleagues? They'd been roommates with a few unimpressive benefits.

The first message was broken up, something about a showing, and Robert would love to be her date for the evening. He was pleased about something.

Huh? If Robert said he was pleased for her, and using that eager, conspiratorial tone, then he was pleased for himself.

Delete. Delete. Delete.

The train pulled into the station, a subterranean dungeon of modern engineering and urban efficiency. Louise stepped onto the platform and extended the handle on her rainbow suitcase. New York was a place that moved forward at a dash not a dawdle, and Louise was moving with it.

Delete Georgia, delete lawyering, delete regrets. Maybe delete the entire USA except for the occasional visit. Good-bye to all of it; hello, creativity, courage, and happiness. Louise came up the escalator, into the regular chaos of the station, and there, standing motionless in the middle of it all, was Liam.

He'd worn a kilt, the colorful clan tartan he'd worn to climb Arthur's Seat with her. For a moment, Louise simply beheld him, a calm, handsome guy oblivious to the few glances his attire earned.

Louise rolled right up to him, dropped the handle of her suitcase, and threw her arms around him.

"I love you, Liam Cromarty."

His arms came around her, slowly. "I beg your pardon?"

No regrets, no looking back, no waiting around for good fortune to sprinkle some random luck her way.

"I love you, Liam Cromarty. I've enjoyed every moment I've spent in your company, and I'm very glad you're here. I brought you some sambusas."

"Sambusas are good, if they're not too spicy."

His embrace was desperately snug—and dear—while his words were tentative.

"Relax, Cromarty. When I say I love you, I'm stating a fact that makes me happy. I'm not handing out a pass/fail quiz for you to complete. Let's get out of this noise, and out of our clothes."

Liam turned loose of Louise enough to grab the handle of her suitcase, but kept an arm around her shoulders.

"Aye to both. The sooner, the better."

* * *

Louise's lovemaking had changed in only a few weeks, become more passionate and tender, more lyrical and demanding. Her very walk had changed, from a businesslike gait to an open stride that said she knew exactly where she was going.

She loved him. If Liam had doubted Louise's words, he could not doubt her actions. As she wrestled Liam over her and wiggled her way beneath him, her smooth, warm curves, and strong hands eased aches in his heart even before they'd tended to other aches.

"You've missed me, then?" Liam asked, kissing her cheek. He could wallow in the simple scent of her.

"Desperately. How about if we screw like bunnies now and save the romantic stuff for later? This is Manhattan. We can have Eritrean delivered with a side of Thai fusion and designer ice cream chaser."

A sure recipe for indigestion.

"We'll compromise," Liam said, angling his head to take a nipple between his teeth. "We'll be romantic bunnies."

Louise retaliated by grabbing his bum in a potter's very firm grasp, and his hair, and kissing him witless while she wrapped her legs around him and muttered about how he'd better have brought her some tablet.

"I brought you tablet," Liam said, levering up onto his elbows. "I've brought you all manner of sweets, including,"—in one hard, sure thrust, he ended their mutual teasing—"this. God, I've missed you."

They went still for a moment, smiling at each other. Liam needed to see that same smile on Louise's face when the evening ended, too. The thought helped him hold back, helped him impersonate a very romantic, hopelessly besotted rabbit who'd do anything for his lady.

Except change their plans for the evening.

Louise was asleep, her head in Liam's lap, when his phone chimed six-thirty. Outside, the ceaseless screech, thump, and horn blasts of traffic had shifted from the day to the evening song of the city, and the sun was taking its light away.

"Wake up, love," Liam whispered, tousling Louise's hair. "Time for bright lights, big city."

Time to risk everything on the hope that they had a future. A better man would have spent the afternoon sightseeing with her, but Liam simply hadn't been able to. Louise had lived in New York for several years. She didn't need another visit to Rockefeller Plaza, not as badly as Liam needed to have her to himself.

Possibly for one last time.

"Sleep," Louise muttered, nuzzling at him. Thank goodness the sheets came between her cheek and his equipment, because she'd already proved her mouth was a powerful weapon against his best intentions.

"No more of your tricks, Louise Cameron. We need sustenance."

"Carryout."

Any other night with her, in any other city, even in this city. "I brought my Highland dress regalia, and by God you'll help me into it."

Her head came up. "The fussy kilt? With the jacket and vest and knee socks?"

"The very one, though I can still stash some tablet in my sporran." A dress sporran, complete with tassels and silver trim.

Liam explained each piece of the full outfit and affixed his *sgian-dubh* to his left calf, because the evening ought to be a hospitable outing. The only other sharp knife in evidence might be the one Louise would take to his heart.

Liam's cell phone had been quiet for once, an encouraging sign.

When he was properly attired in formal Highland dress, Louise shimmied into a dark green silk sheath that was lovely, but not half so intriguing to Liam as her shimmying.

"Down, laddie," he muttered in the direction of his sporran.

"Will you get the hook at the top of my zipper?" Louise asked, turning her back and sweeping her hair off her nape. The engagement ring Liam had brought with him would go wonderfully with her dress—an encouraging omen, surely.

Liam obliged, though fastening the small hook and eye took several tries. "You'll wear your hair down?"

"Not quite, but give me five minutes for some lip gloss and eyeliner, and I'll be ready to go."

Hotel rooms in New York were priced in proportion to their square footage, and Liam had not splurged on a penthouse. Preparing for the evening together had an extra intimacy because of the cozy quarters, and because getting dressed up for a night on the town was another new, shared experience for them.

A vision in green and grace emerged from the bathroom. The dress made Louise's natural movements shimmer and slide, and she'd done something with her hair—left it cascading over one shoulder, not up, not down. All manner of curving lines, from her hips to her shoulders, to her knees, danced as she moved.

"I don't believe I've ever seen you in heels," Liam said. Inane remark, but it made her smile.

"These are low heels. I can stand around in them all night, but only you would notice a lady's shoes."

The shoes were a seafoamy green and sparkly, like magic slippers. Gold dangled from Louise's earlobes, and a single jade teardrop hung from a gold chain right above her cleavage.

"I wish, for the first time in my life, that I could paint," Liam said. "We'd need a bed in my studio, though."

"If you keep talking like that, we'll never get to the restaurant," Louise replied, Georgia swaying through her vowels. She picked up a gold clutch purse from the night table and the vision of luscious, relaxed sophistication was complete.

Seven fifteen on the nose. "I've reservations at eight," Liam said, not exactly a lie. "Not far from here, in fact."

"Then lay on, Cromarty, because somebody helped me work up an appetite."

Liam was the envy of every man who saw them, and he'd never had such quick luck hailing a New York cab. As he handed Louise in, and gave the cabby directions, Liam prayed his luck would hold for the rest of the night.

* * *

A student could live in New York for several years and not learn much more of the town than the nearest cheap restaurants, a couple of suds-yer-duds, and a half-dozen coffee shops. Louise had fared a little better than that, but not much.

"Is this restaurant one of your favorites?" Louise asked as Liam handed her out of the cab.

"I hope you'll like this place," Liam said, winging his arm at her, though nobody walked down the street in New York arm in arm.

What did that matter? Louise took Liam's arm, though they were in the skyscraper canyons of the Financial District. By day, all would be sunlight reflecting off of new construction, and bustling crowds of sharply-dressed professionals exuding stress and self-importance in equal measure.

"In here," Liam said, gesturing to a discrete, formal façade in the middle of a block. A limousine waited by the curb.

Maybe the restaurant was in the basement or on the roof?

Louise walked with Liam past a reception area where a guard at a desk asked for their names. Louise was too busy studying the frescoes and paintings on the walls to pay much attention.

"This place is gorgeous," she said, when Liam would have hauled her over to the elevators. "Can you imagine what that stained glass looks like in daylight?"

"It's magnificent," Liam said, "and the patterns the window glass makes on the floor on a sunny afternoon are intended to dance with the inlays on the tiles. We'll come back and admire it someday."

A note in his voice caught Louise's attention. They'd have a someday, a lot of somedays, of that Louise was increasingly certain. She didn't need pretty words when she had that steady, tender regard in Liam's blue eyes.

"Let's go to dinner," she said, taking Liam's hand. "We'll do the Met tomorrow, assuming I let you out of bed."

"We'll do the Met," Liam answered, kissing her on the mouth. "Or whatever you please."

He was dangerously good-looking in his finery, not simply because he was a handsome guy. He knew *how* to wear Highland formal attire, knew exactly where the sporran ought to rest, knew the feel of the kilt draped against his thighs.

"I still want to sketch you," Louise murmured as they stepped off the elevator. "Without your clothes, Liam."

They were in another lobby of sorts, a mezzanine space that stretched for much of the floor. People milled about here, and to one side of the area, a buffet had been set up.

The flowers along the buffet were gorgeous without being too showy. Purples and greens with the occasional dash of yellow or red.

"Liam? This does not look like a restaurant." It looked like a reception...

or a *showing*. Louise's gaze returned to the flowers, beautiful, understated and vaguely disquieting.

"There's plenty to eat," Liam said. "I made sure of that, and the bar's in that corner. Let's have a look at the main attraction, though, shall we?"

Restaurants did not have main attractions. One of Louise's former professors, a woman who'd done quite well with textiles, waggled her fingers at Louise and disquiet threatened to coalesce into anxiety.

"Robert's here," Louise said, her middle abruptly recalling the bleak feel of Culloden Battlefield. "I never wanted to see him again, Liam. Why would you ask me to get all dressed up just so you could take me someplace where I'd have to deal with *him*?"

And God help her, Larry O'Connor, the grand old man of studio art reviews was over at the bar.

"Robert has come to practice his skills as a hanger-on," Liam said. "The show is public, so I couldn't keep him out even after what Jane had to say about him when I interrogated her yesterday. You needn't speak to him, but you might enjoy his groveling."

Through a set of glass and chrome double doors, somebody moved and Louise caught a flash of a tall vase on a white stand. All manner of blues and greens blended and swirled in the glazes, gold lurked at the edge of every color, and light seemed to pour from the surface.

"Liam Cromarty, what have you done?"

O'Connor waved, a jovial little troll of a man who'd spoken to Louise's classes about art criticism throughout history.

"I have put right a wrong I did nearly a decade ago," Liam said.

His hold on Louise's hand was all that kept her from bolting for the elevators.

"You're not an art critic," Louise said, her heart feeling the pull of the blue and green vase, and whatever else might be behind those double doors. "You have nothing to do with why I went to law school."

"I had everything to do with it, Louise. I was among those Saxe hauled to your showing, to sneer at and ridicule student works, some of which were brilliant. The phrase 'major in Teacher's Pet' originated with me, as did other disparaging remarks. Even as I uttered them, I was baffled at how a student, an undergraduate struggling to emulate her more experienced teacher, could so thoroughly surpass his results."

Liam had both hands wrapped around Louise's fingers. "Then the next morning, I saw my own words in print," he went on, "casual, snide, half-drunken comments meant only for a small, snide, half-drunken group. That day was a turning point for me, the lowest point in a long, stupid fall from decency and self-respect. I am sorry, Louise. The harm was unintentional, but entirely my fault. Do you accept my apology?"

Two thoughts crowded into Louise's mind, the first was that Liam needed to shut up. Whatever he was blathering about, they could discuss later.

The second thought, more of a compulsion, was that her best work, her very best work, properly displayed before a segment of New York's most discerning appreciators of art, lay beyond the doors.

She didn't give a damn about the people, but her art—

"I want to see," she said, dragging Liam across the room. "I have to see them."

Liam went peacefully, a few people calling greetings. When they reached the double doors, Louise was abruptly, unashamedly terrified. She buried her face against Liam's throat, his lacy jabot tickling her cheek.

"I thought they'd been d-destroyed," she whispered. "I asked for them back, from the galleries that had agreed to take them on commission, though it took me weeks to find the nerve. They all said the pieces were 'no longer in inventory.' I got a check, when what I wanted was my art back. I've always wanted my art back. I thought they'd all gone in d-dumpsters—"

"Look, Louise," Liam said softly, arms around her. "Every piece is whole and safe, and they're all here, except for one vase that I sent to a friend drowning in grief."

Louise couldn't hold on to Liam tightly enough, could not contain the singing, soaring joy, or the terror, of what he'd done.

"Show me, Liam."

An attendant opened the double doors, and Liam escorted her into a carpeted expanse of light and quiet. Her best work—vases, bowls, a whimsical teapot, a fan made of clay and northern lights, a dish wide enough to serve as a grinding stone, a matched set of tea cups…. Every piece accounted for, every piece perfectly lit to show off form and finish.

Louise knew which one Liam had sent to his friend: A vase about six inches tall that she'd named Consolation. In this room, Liam had assembled all of the rest. Her past, her future, her heart, all on display.

"They're beautiful," Louise said, wiping a tear away with the back of her wrist. "I was never sure. I thought maybe I'd not seen clearly, maybe memory played tricks, maybe merely pretty is all I'm capable of."

"You're capable of gorgeous, insightful, brilliant work, all of it," Liam said. "Not a runt in the litter, Louise Cameron, not a second best, not a single item that falls below the standard of the rest. You're not only a genius with color and shape, you're consistent. Larry O'Connor agreed when he was given a private showing this morning."

Louise leaned into Liam and wept, and she laughed, and she dreamed up all manner of new shapes and approaches to try. She was still giddy with sheer joy two hours later as the attendants began to discreetly murmur about the bar closing soon, and there being time for one last trip to the buffet.

"I don't want to leave this room, Liam," Louise said as she accepted a piece of tablet from him. "*I made this*, I made all of this, and it's good." She kissed him as sweetness suffused her. "You know what else, Cromarty? *I can make more.* I know that now. Purple is calling to me, like the heather. Purple and green have a lot to say to each other."

And Louise had more she'd say to Liam, when all these smiling, well-dressed people left them some privacy.

"Let's find a glass of champagne," Liam suggested, "because this was a successful show if ever I saw one."

"Larry O'Connor winked at me," Louise said, slipping out of her shoes as the textile artist waved good-bye. Louise was tipsy, though she'd not had even a glass of wine. "I want you to understand something, though, Liam Cromarty."

Liam collected her shoes. "Say my name like that in bed. You'll like the results."

He led her from the display room to the bar. Louise waited for their drinks while Liam found a place to stash her shoes.

"I feel like we should waltz on the roof or something," Louise said, passing Liam his champagne. She touched her glass to his. "To Scotland, the brave."

Liam kissed her, then took a sip, and set the drink aside. "I asked you earlier if you accepted my apology, Louise. May I take it you've responded in the affirmative?"

* * *

Louise had become like one of her vases, a pillar of grace and beauty, illuminated from within, imbued with motion even when she stood still.

"Let's find some ferns to hide behind," she said, taking Liam by the hand. "Understand this: You are being daft, and I love you for it, but enough is enough."

"I am daft," Liam said as they wound past the buffet and into a conversational grouping away from the brightest lights. Across the mezzanine, people were putting on wraps, security guards were looking relieved, and a wonderfully successful show was coming to an end.

The press had attended, and Liam would have a few more clients for this evening's work, about which, he cared not at all.

"I was mean to Robert," Louise said, stretching luxuriously.

"You were quite civil to him," Liam countered, lowering himself to the carpet beside her chair. "You asked about his latest publication then dodged off to say hello to the reigning queen of textile art."

Larry O'Connor had been trapped in a discussion of the symbolism of fur in colonial portraiture for another fifteen minutes while Liam had stayed at his lady's side.

"Naughty me," Louise said, admiring her own bare toes.

She could light up the Orkneys on New Year's Eve with that smile.

"Might I interrupt your naughtiness to trouble you for your opinion on another artist's work?" Liam asked.

Louise stroked his hair, the gentlest caress. "I'd give you pretty much anything you asked for, Liam Cromarty. I hadn't realized how I'd been grieving, not knowing what had happened to my art. Without the actual pieces, I had no evidence I'd ever created anything. Thank you from the bottom of my heart. The managing partner for the law firm that hosted this shindig asked if I accepted private commissions."

"You'll soon be wealthy if you said yes." And how pleased Liam would be, to see Louise's career restored to her in such abundance.

Louise dropped a kiss on his crown. "I am wealthy. I have good health, a ton of ideas, and good people in my life. The rest doesn't matter."

She didn't reiterate that she loved him. She'd lobbed that salvo at him when he'd been too drunk on the sight of her to respond, and then she'd nattered on about taking his clothes off.

Liam scooted around, so he was on his knees at her side. "You have something else, too, Louise."

"A sweet tooth. Or a tablet tooth."

"You have my heart," Liam said, extracting a ring box from a pocket. "You have my love. You have my loyalty, my fidelity, and most of my tablet stash for the rest of my natural days. My cat and my uncle have already switched their allegiance to you, and my dog is sure to follow."

Louise had gone still, her hand resting on his shoulder.

"Thank you, Liam. I love you, too. Very much."

"We thought we were done," he said. "You went off to law school, thinking you'd closed a chapter in your life forever. I settled into teaching and hoped I could be content. I don't want contentment, Louise, unless I can share it with you." He passed her the ring box. "What do you think of the setting?"

Louise opened the box and peered at the ring as if it might jump up and bite her nose. Liam kissed that nose instead.

"Will it do, Louise? Will I do?"

"Oh, Liam. Of course you'll do, but may I have the words, please?"

He assumed a proper kneeling posture. "Louise Cameron, will you marry me? Will you become my lawfully wedded wife, my best friend, my partner, lover, and companion in all things? I come with a lot of family and a stubborn streak."

She looped her arms around his shoulders. "Stubborn is good, Liam. Stubborn means we don't give up, we keep trying, we find a way to make our marriage work. I'll marry you, and you'll have a stubborn wife, too."

A yes, then. A beautiful, heartfelt, unhesitating yes. Louise had said yes to him, to his love, to a shared future. Liam stuffed the ring box in his pocket and slid the gold band around Louise's finger.

"I love it," she said, wiggling her fingers so the light caught the emerald.

"I love you." Liam had waited weeks to say that, the longest weeks of his life. "I love you, I love you. I love you, and I want an early wedding present."

"I gave you some early wedding presents this afternoon, Liam Cromarty."

Had she ever. Liam drew Louise to her feet. "And what lovely gestures those were. Now I want another kind of lovely gesture."

The recessed lighting around the mezzanine had dimmed, and staff were clearing off the buffet.

"Will I need my shoes?" Louise asked as Liam led her back to the display area.

"Not for this. I want a guided tour, Louise. I want to hear the story of each piece, to know what decisions you had to make, where the ideas came from, and what comes next."

"I know what comes next," she said, stopping before a loving cup with braided handles. The lights had been turned down in here too, and yet, the greens and golds of the glaze seemed to glow with warmth. "What comes next, Liam Cromarty, is we live happily ever after."

EPILOGUE

Every artist needed a spouse, a Liam Cromarty, to handle all the pesky financial details associated with sales, to offer the occasional—though never unsolicited—comment on a work in progress, and to impersonate a romantic bunny several times throughout the day.

Liam had the knack of leaving Louise alone her in studio precisely long enough to accomplish a goal, but not long enough for her to grow hungry or unproductive. He was often at work elsewhere in the house, grading papers, preparing for class, or transacting art rental business with clients a dozen time zones away.

Or, when the mood struck, cooking.

"You made sambusas," Louise said, snatching a clean towel from the stack near the work sink. "What do you want to bet Uncle Donald will be here in the next fifteen minutes?"

Liam set down a tray laden with a pile of golden, flakey sambusas, two bottles of Deuchars beer, and a roll of paper towels.

"Donald is off working on his golf game," Liam said. "Seems another one of your lawyer friends from Maryland has decided to come to Scotland for a golfing holiday."

Louise opened both bottles, taking a sniff of hop-py loveliness.

"The only lawyers in Maryland I'd call my friends are Dunstan and Jane." Mostly Jane, though Dunstan had grown on her. "I certainly know a few more, and most of them are decent people."

None of whom she missed.

Liam took a sip of his beer, and what did it say about a woman who'd been married for nearly two months, that she still found the sight of her husband *drinking beer* sexy?

Liam passed her two sambusas on a paper towel. "Shame on you. You know better than to look at me like that, Mrs. Cromarty."

Mrs. Cromarty. She was Louise Cameron Cromarty now, soon to be a master's degree candidate at the Glasgow School of Art. She and Liam had decided to first take a year to enjoy being married, and for Louise to settle into her Scottish home.

A fine plan, but like all plans…

"That's a lovely piece," Liam said, gesturing with his bottle at a pot Louise had taken from the kiln earlier in the day. "You meant what you said, about purple and green having a lot to say to each other, and the peach goes surprisingly well."

Louise took a bite of food still warm from the oven. "This is your best recipe yet. If you give it to Donald, he might leave us alone for more than three days at a time."

Though Louise knew why Donald was stopping by so often. Auld Donald was a canny fellow.

"A fine notion," Liam said, chewing contemplatively.

Marriage had changed him, added peacefulness to his quiet, and smiles to his conversation. Louise was about to upset that quiet, but also, she hoped, to inspire more smiles.

"Who's the next guest in the cottage?" she asked. "The bar association was full of golfers, though I had the sense they played mostly to get out of the office."

Niall Cromarty was the family golfer and Jeannie's brother. He had Liam's broad shoulders, also a thriving little golf operation in the wilds of Perthshire, and form most pros could only envy.

Niall did not, however, lay claim to any charm.

"The next guest," Liam said, "is a lady by the name of Julie Leonard. She's quite focused on her golf apparently."

For a prosecutor, Julie had been pleasant to work with. "*Niall's* supposed to brave the midgies to take her golfing?"

"Which is why Jeannie sent Donald off to the links. One must always have a backup plan. I don't suppose you play?"

Plans again. *Please, Liam, be the kind of husband who can adjust to a change in plans.*

"I don't play golf worth a hoot," Louise said. "Niall might not make a bad golf buddy for Julie." Who was used to dealing with trial attorneys and criminals.

"He'll be awful," Liam said, finishing his first sambusa. "Niall's in want of cheer, unless you happen to be a drooling, cooing wee bairnie by the name of Henry."

Louise set her beer down after one sip. Deuchars had become her favorite, but she wouldn't be drinking much for the foreseeable future.

"Everybody can use a devoted uncle," Louise said, "or first cousin once removed."

Liam paused, his bottle halfway to his mouth, while Louise's heart turned over. She would recall this moment, just as she recalled the moment Liam had confused her for a little old lady at the airport. She had an entire mental portfolio of images of Liam, each one beloved. Arthur's Seat, Culloden, walking the banks of the river with Helen, their wedding day.

And their wedding night.

"Niall's first cousins once removed would be… *our children*," Liam said, peering at Louise.

"Got it in one, Mr. Cromarty. Don't suppose you've given any thought to names?"

Liam set his ale down carefully. "Louise?"

"That name's taken, and wouldn't work for a boy."

"Louise Cameron Cromarty. I've wondered what the change is. Your pots have gone from beautiful to sublime, and I didn't think holy matrimony the entire explanation."

The explanation sat across from her, smiling the sweetest, dearest, *hottest* smile.

"Expectant mothers nap a lot," Louise said. "I don't want to nap alone."

Liam grabbed the plate and both beers and nearly ran for the kitchen. Louise beat him to the bedroom, where they did, indeed, enjoy a nice long nap.

Eventually.

–THE END–

To my dear Readers,

I've fallen in love with Scotland, so much so that in September 2016, I'm taking a group of avid readers and aspiring writers on a ten-day tour of some of my favorite Scottish sights. If you're interested in grabbing one of the few slots left, please email me at graceburrowes@yahoo.com, and use "Scotland with Grace" as your subject line. You can also learn more about the planned itinerary on my website, graceburrowes.com.

If you enjoyed these **Two Wee Drams of Love**, you might also like the successor novella duet, **Must Love Scotland**, which includes **Love on the Links** and **My Heartthrob's in the Highlands**. **Love on the Links** features Niall Cromarty, a Scottish pro golfer, and Julie Leonard, an American attorney who hopes that improving her golf game will give her a leg up in the competition for a judgeship. Niall has ambitions for his golf course, Julie has dreams of wearing a black robe… though Niall would love for her to wear his ring instead.

In **My Heartthrob's in the Highlands**, Julie's sister, Megan Leonard, a professional florist, has come to Scotland for Niall and Julie's wedding, but gets tangled up with best man Declan MacPherson. Declan farms the land his family has owned for centuries, while Megan's flower shop, after years of struggle, is now poised to expand. How can love bloom, when an ocean separates the lovers from their happily ever after?

Must Love Scotland is available in print on Amazon.com.

I delight in setting romances in contemporary Scotland, but I've also written historical Scottish romances, including the MacGregor series, set in the Victorian Highlands. Those titles are, in order:

1. The Bridegroom Wore Plaid
2. Once Upon a Tartan
3. The MacGregor's Lady
4. What A Lady Needs for Christmas

Tantor Media offers the first three of those titles on audio at tantormedia.com.

I love to hear from my readers, so please feel free to reach me through my website at graceburrowes.com, or on Facebook as Grace Burrowes, an on twitter through @graceburrowes.

Haste ye back and happy reading!
Grace Burrowes

19108566R00090

Printed in Great Britain
by Amazon